S0-DMV-266

Endorsements for *Lie Cheat Steal*

This book had unexpected twists and turns with unbelievable stories! It was awesome!
—Alli Renken, age eleven

In this day of standardized tests that don't seem to have a clue about young people and their experience of school, how refreshing to hear the diverse voices of his students and get their "take" on things. This book is going to be loved by the cool kids and the nerds (like me) for years to come!
—Emily Hayden, PhD, assistant professor, literacy education, Iowa State University

Honest and emotional. *Lie, Cheat, Steal* is amazing! Mr. C is documenting what is real. Try to put it down ... I dare you!
—Sheri Christen, media specialist

Mr. C writes so brilliantly that it entertains both teachers and students. Highlighting the true moments of school, but also using such captivating language will keep kids (and parents and teachers) laughing while also learning. A must-read for your read-alouds.
—Megan Kuehl, classroom teacher

written by JEFF CHARTIER

&

illustrated by P. BRADLEY

INFUSIONMEDIA
Lincoln, Nebraska

© 2021 Jeff Chartier. All rights reserved.

No part of this publication may be reproduced, distributed, or transmitted in any form or by any means, including photocopying, recording, digital scanning, or other electronic or mechanical methods, without the prior written permission of the copyright holder, except in the case of brief quotations embodied in critical reviews and certain other noncommercial uses permitted by copyright law.

Infusionmedia
2124 Y St, #138
Lincoln, NE 68503
https://infusion.media
#attheflats

Printed in the United States

10 9 8 7 6 5 4 3 2 1
First Edition

ISBN: 978-1-945834-22-6
Library of Congress Control Number: 2021908074

Illustrations by P. Bradley

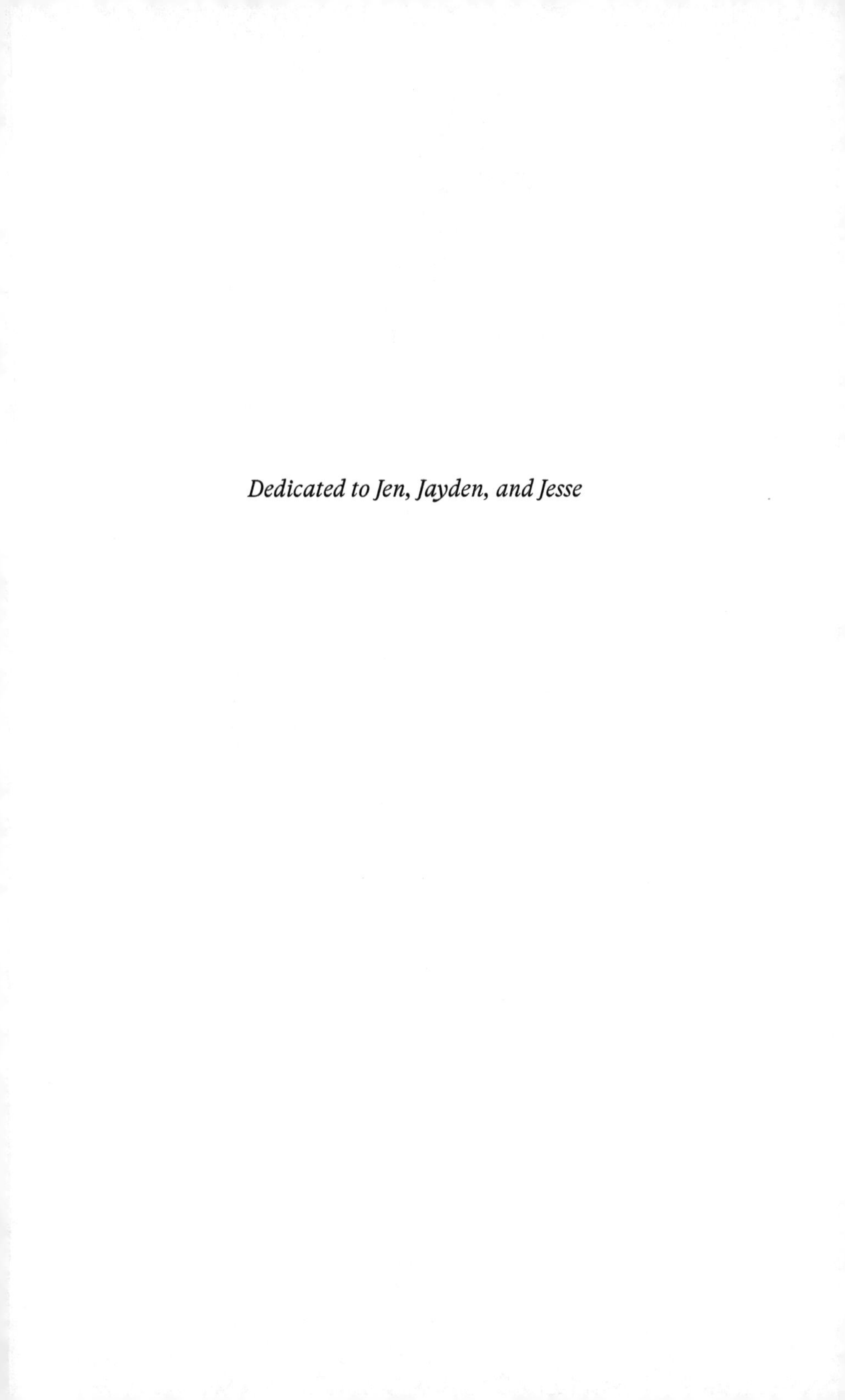

Dedicated to Jen, Jayden, and Jesse

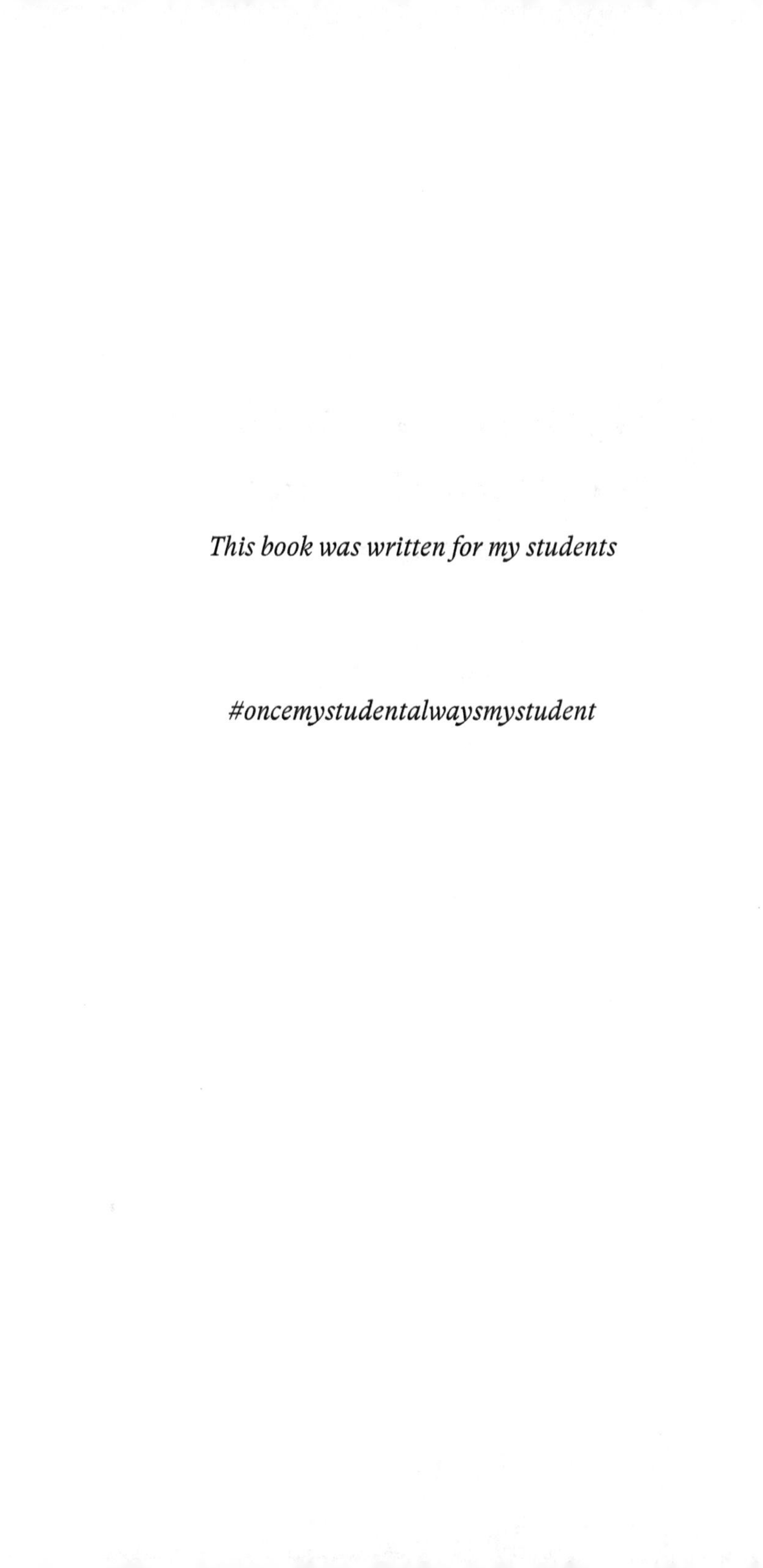

This book was written for my students

#oncemystudentalwaysmystudent

"If you don't see the book you want on the shelves, write it."

—Beverly Cleary

CONTENTS

YOU DON'T KNOW WHAT YOU DON'T KNOW

I don't know what your school is like,
but mine is captivating, to say the least.
There are lots of crazy things that happen.
Everything from beauty to the beast.

I've seen and heard a lot of things.
That always comes with a price.
Those things that make a parent cringe,
I've seen and heard it twice.

The school that I attend
is one of "those" kinds of schools.
We're known for low test scores
and students disobeying the rules.

We're the school from "that" side of town.
Don't let your imagination go too far.
It's time to get this monkey off our back.
We're the school *where the wild things are...*

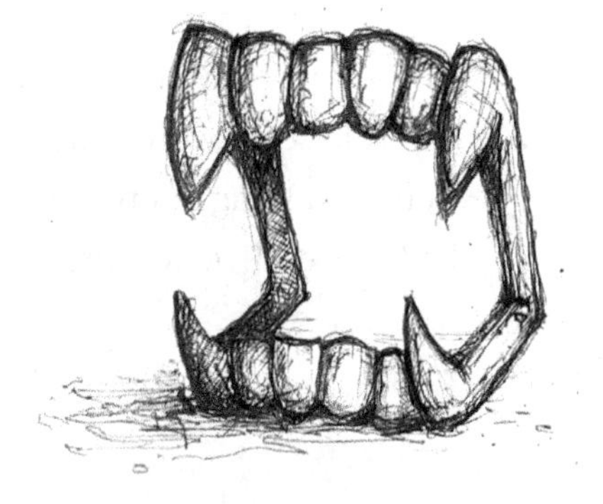

Another school day was about to start.
The bell hadn't even rung.
Mr. C was greeting students at the door
when a student had a slip of the tongue.

I'm not easily offended.
Bad language doesn't bother me at all.
Before he came into our classroom,
he was bullying students in the hall.

Sometimes when he comes into class
he's just looking to stir the pot.
He makes learning hard for everybody.
He's naughty ... he does this stuff a lot!

Mr. C walked over to the student
and said, "Please go work in room 219."
That's the room naughty kids go to work
when they're disruptive or they're mean.

The Future Felon tried to lie.
Then he asked for one more chance.
Mr. C said that's not an option.
It was always the same old song and dance.

The Future Felon kicked over his chair
and said some words I'd never heard.
Before walking out the door,
he flipped Mr. C the bird!

Mr. C stayed very calm.
I think he was trying not to laugh.
What he said next was savage.
I think I want his autograph.

"I'm honored you think I'm number one.
I thought you'd think I was mean.
Please don't forget your assignment.
Now, will you please go to room 219?"

The Future Felon was befuddled,
that finger still pointed at Mr. C.
So he flipped him the bird with both hands!
Two birds not found in a tree.

We didn't see that coming.
No one knew what to think.
We sat in awkward silence.
Mr. C didn't even blink.

"Double number one?
We can't sweep this under the rug.
Before you go to room 219,
bring it in and give me a hug!"

The Future Felon would have none of that.
He bolted out the door.
I'm not sure if he made it to 219, but
I don't think we'll see those birds anymore!

Two birds had flown the coop.
Birds that are not supposed to fly.
A feather in the hand
is better than two birds in the sky.

You'd think that would be enough excitement,
but we're actually just getting started.
What happens next in this story
is not for the weak or fainthearted!

Our class got back on track
to our *rigorous learning* life.
We heard a teacher in the hall.
She said there's a student with a knife!

My imagination ran wild.
I think my heart just skipped a beat.
Then I heard a siren outside.
The police are coming down the street!

Our school went into lockdown
to keep the student's protected.
I know what you may be thinking.
The Future Felon is connected.

We all rushed to the window
to see what's going down.
Channel 8 news had just arrived.
There was a reporter on the playground.

I was expecting to see chaos
like a horror movie slasher scene.
A knife-wielding *Future Felon*
in a movie rated NC-17.

If this were a movie,
it would be as BORING as could be!
Nobody would go see it,
and it would probably be rated G.

We saw a student from our class.
He's just a really *nice guy*.
He was with the principal and a cop?
I didn't think he could hurt a fly!

As we watched the story unfold,
it made less and less sense.
We didn't see anybody with a knife.
Our questions were immense!

An announcement was made
that said the lockdown had ended.
Did The Nice Guy really have a knife?
Do you think he'll get suspended?

How are we supposed to focus
with all these questions hanging in the air?
The Future Felon, The Nice Guy, a knife?
Visitors to our school, beware!

Maybe he was being bullied.
There are some scary kids in our school.
Scarier than The Future Felon.
They don't abide by the golden rule.

Mr. C said sometimes a story
is nothing but a ruse.
You can't judge a book by its cover
until you walk a day in their shoes.

I'm not saying Mr. C is wrong,
but this is a lot on our plate.
Do other schools deal with this kind of stuff?
Mr. C's statement might be up for debate.

As I glanced back out the window,
I saw a familiar face.
It was The Nice Guy's mom.
She was walking at a very fast pace.

She's a helicopter mom
who appears to be on a mission.
Her nickname is The Viper.
Expect a thorough inquisition!

Our principal rolls her eyes
whenever The Viper comes to school.
I've seen her make teachers cry,
which is not the golden rule.

The Viper is clearly agitated.
We can't hear what she's saying.
I know this is a public school ... BUT
someone may want to start praying!

The Viper is a member
of a team that is extreme.
They're the Mad Momma Militia.
They always have a scheme.

She thinks her son is perfect
and nothing is ever his fault.
If he earns a bad grade,
it's an all-out teacher assault!

The Viper likes to point fingers
when things don't go her way.
She got our last principal fired,
though that is just hearsay.

I know our school has problems.
I bet yours does as well.
We'll get answers, hook or by crook.
It's a mystery we need to dispel.

As for Mr. C and The Viper,
they haven't clashed as of yet.
The Viper just walked into our class.
This could be the day he gets his feet wet.

The Viper looked angry.
She's as cold as ice.
She has Resting Grumpy Face.
How is her son so really REALLY nice?

Our principal has also arrived.
They are both talking to Mr. C.
We were eavesdropping as best we could.
They were whispering ... it's hard to be nosey!

Our principal looked frazzled,
which I guess you can't blame her.
The Viper is doing most of the talking.
She's a downright gangster!

As if today wasn't strange enough,
The Nice Guy came walking in.
He was carrying a box,
a clue to an unexpected spin.

That's when it hit me
like a right hook from left field.
A lightbulb went off in my head.
The answer will soon be revealed.

The Nice Guy wasn't holding a knife,
but I think it's safe to assume.
A crazy train has gone off the rails.
I bet the knife is here in this room!

I've pieced this puzzle together,
a Nice Guy paradox.
He's holding the final piece,
and I know what's in that box!

We assaulted him with questions.
The Nice Guy was on the spot.
The ball is in his court.
It's time to take a shot.

The Nice Guy was overwhelmed.
He normally doesn't have much to say.
With three words it all made sense.
He said, "It's my birthday."

The silence was deafening
as we processed what he'd said.
The Nice Guy is in fact just that,
but we can't put this story to bed.

I know this story seems crazy.
I promise this story isn't fake.
This puzzle is almost complete.
He needed a knife to cut the cake.

The Nice Guy had come to school early.
He wanted to surprise the class with cake.
The Nice Guy forgot to bring a knife.
That's when he made a BIG mistake!

The Nice Guy ran home and got a knife.
His intentions were good at heart.
He was running back to school ... WITH A KNIFE!
Hindsight is 20/20 ... that was not smart!

Someone saw The Nice Guy running,
and they called 911.
The Nice Guy was also late for school.
His birthday had not been very fun!

A teacher saw him coming,
radioed the office he was running late.
She told them the student had a knife,
prompting a neighbor to call Channel 8.

She'd been listening on a police scanner,
eavesdropping on the conversation.
A nosey neighbor stirring the pot.
It exposed her covert operation.

A student wielding a knife.
A headline story with juice.
That's when everyone showed up.
We "thought" all hell would break loose!

Our school didn't make the news.
The police knew it was a mistake.
The only question left unanswered was...
Who was going to cut the cake?

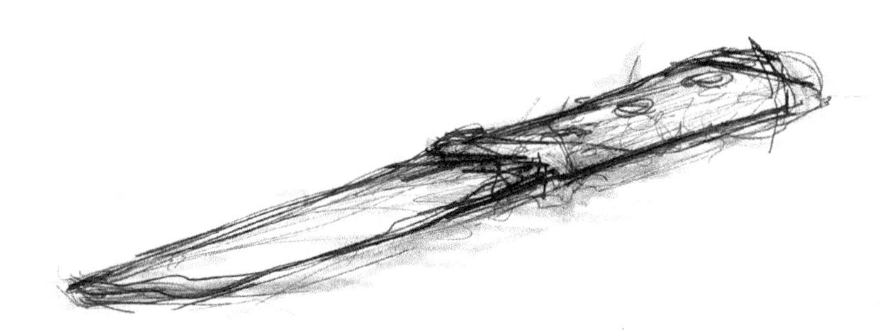

Our reputation precedes us.
It's done so at our expense.
Truth is stranger than fiction
because fiction has to make sense!

HONOR

AMONG THIEVES

I'm REALLY disappointed.
Not sure where to start.
My teacher has decided
we need a new seating chart?

I hate when this happens.
This never goes well.
Now I sit by The Fiend,
and he's meaner than hell!

I begged to be moved.
The teacher ignored my plea.
She said I'm a good influence.
Now The Fiend sits by me!

So help me understand.
My knowledge is minimal.
Because I do my job
I get to sit by a criminal?

So I did what I do.
I smiled and complied.
I've got a bad feeling,
but I have to abide.

This is my story.
I am quiet and shy.
If you ask me to do something,
I'll never ask why.

I don't have many friends.
I'm kind of an outcast.
If you're picking a team,
you'll be picking me last.

My parents always tell me
I'm smart and I'm pretty.
My teachers all like me
because I'm on every committee.

I always know the answers,
as my teachers will attest.
My teachers all love me
because I aced the state test.

I never get Snapchats
or invited to the mall.
Nobody is mean to me.
I'm just another brick in the wall.

I complained to my parents.
They said I might do him some good.
They said give him a chance.
Maybe he's just misunderstood.

Let me tell you about this *student*,
and I use that word loosely.
He's insidious and hideous.
He cusses profusely.

He never does homework,
and he loves to interrupt.
If you ask him a question,
he'll tell you to shut the @#*% up!

I tried my best to explain
what school is REALLY like.
My explanation fell on deaf ears.
Are kids allowed to go on strike?

They said talk to your teacher,
which I already did.
They said no kid can be that bad.
I'm about to flip my lid!

I went back and talked to my teacher,
which was a total waste of time.
She mostly ignored me.
My teacher said I'd be just fine.

Her interests were elsewhere.
She was checking her phone.
She hides it in her desk,
which is something I've known.

So I did what I do,
I smiled and complied.
I've got a bad feeling,
but I have to abide.

It started in math.
The Fiend likes to provoke.
He started picking his nose.
I'm serious ... that isn't a joke!

He blew on my paper
so it fell to the ground.
I asked him to please stop.
He called me a hound.

During independent reading,
he passed me a note.
It said everyone hates me.
The class took a vote.

He poked me and mocked me.
The Fiend is really weird.
The teacher didn't see anything.
My homework disappeared.

The Fiend has some issues,
and that's quite apparent.
The teacher's constantly praising him.
It's very transparent.

When the teacher isn't looking,
he's asking me to cheat.
He just whispered something
I could never repeat.

There's good news for me.
I've had about all I can take!
The Fiend is leaving our class
for his first assigned *Movement Break?*

The principal comes in.
The Fiend gets his coat.
He gets extra recess.
I'm serious ... that isn't a joke!

I know what they're doing.
They're building up his self-esteem.
This is totally unfair.
This has to be a dream!

For twenty minutes
at least three times a day,
I can get a reprieve
while The Fiend goes to play.

Upon his return,
his behaviors are high.
It's hard to stay focused
when the teacher turns a blind eye.

It doesn't add up.
His behaviors are sordid.
The Fiend gets away with murder!
His actions are rewarded!!

The teacher goes out of her way
to help him succeed.
She practically does his work.
I've NEVER seen him read.

When I got home from school,
I was so mad I could scream!
I told my parents everything.
Now they know he's extreme.

That got their attention.
They weren't happy at all.
My dad was furious!
My mom's ready to brawl!

My parents called the principal
early the next day.
They were still up in arms.
They said there'd be hell to pay!

The principal thanked them for the call.
She will investigate my claim.
She's taking this matter seriously.
My principal *talks* a big game.

Later that morning.
It was just before lunch.
I was called to the office.
I think I know why ... call it a hunch.

When I arrived at the office,
the principal was waiting.
She thanked me for coming.
She's kind of intimidating.

"I've talked with your teacher.
I have heard what you've claimed.
The teacher hasn't seen anything.
The student feels framed."

I promised I wasn't lying.
I was telling the truth.
She asked, "Were there any witnesses?
Do you have any proof?"

I was at a loss for words.
There was nothing else I could do.
Maybe she's running late
for movement break number two?

The meeting came to an end.
Nothing was resolved.
Do they really believe
The Fiend wasn't involved?

Now I'm concerned.
The Fiend knows that I told.
If lying were an Olympic sport,
The Fiend would win gold.

When I returned to class,
my teacher said I could move.
Me? Shouldn't it be The Fiend?
At least things should improve.

I shouldn't be surprised.
My problems became more profound.
The Fiend stepped up his game.
He just moved it underground.

The comments continued.
He's not holding back.
They were vile and disgusting.
I'm having a panic attack!

How is it possible
The Fiend never gets caught?
He's been kicked out of two schools.
He's a behavior juggernaut!

My teachers determined
The Fiend does nothing wrong.
While she's drinking his Kool-Aid,
this may be my swan song.

Being scared and a victim
has become a new habit.
I've fallen down a hole,
chasing a white rabbit.

But what I thought was a hole
was actually an escape.
A watershed moment
has just taken shape.

I looked up from that hole,
never admitting defeat.
I let myself be a victim.
It's The Fiend's turn to retreat!

I picked myself up
and dusted myself off.
Call it a paradigm shift.
Now I'm pissed off!

The very next morning
The Fiend got in my face.
I had a card up my sleeve.
The card was an ace.

My teacher was on duty,
again checking her phone.
The Fiend thinks I'm trapped.
He thinks I'm alone.

He raised his fist.
Tried to make me flinch.
I laughed in his face.
I didn't move an inch!

I admit I was scared,
but I didn't bat an eye.
I stood my ground.
The Fiend's plan went awry.

You might be thinking
that I'm not very wise.
What goes around comes around.
He's in for a surprise!

For I could see something
The Fiend couldn't see.
Someone WAS watching.
It was my math teacher ... Mr. C.

The Fiend was dumbfounded.
I'm going to make this sting.
I just took out his queen.
Now I'm going after his king.

The tables have turned.
I'm no longer the pawn.
The Fiend was blindsided.
Now he knows it's game on!

Much to his chagrin,
The Fiend was whisked away.
But I know it's not that easy
to keep a monster at bay.

The Fiend wasn't in class.
"Oh, for goodness sake!"
I looked out the window.
HE STILL GETS A MOVEMENT BREAK?

The Fiend returned to class.
No need to ask why.
He was staring me down.
I must have something in my eye?

I'm after redemption.
I won't let him win.
He's just a paper tiger
with a Cheshire grin.

We had a class project.
I wasn't working alone.
The Fiend's eyes are like daggers.
My teacher is checking her phone.

Every time he came near me,
I went and talked to the teacher.
I made up some questions
that were not beneath her.

It was driving The Fiend crazy.
I stayed two steps ahead.
I have his king trapped.
The Fiend is hanging by a thread.

Amidst all the chaos,
the teacher yelled, *"STOP!"*
Her phone had gone missing.
You could've heard a pin drop.

To say she was in a panic
was easy to assume.
She said until her phone showed up,
NOBODY was leaving the room!

My teacher was furious.
The class was dead quiet.
"I KNOW ONE OF YOU TOOK IT!"
My teacher's ready to riot!

The class was aghast
by the teacher's little fit.
I slowly raised my hand and said,
"Why don't you just call it?"

She said, *"That's a good idea!"*
And I agreed that it was.
As we all sat and listened,
we heard vibrations and a buzz.

The sound was coming
from inside a desk.
I'll give you three guesses who
in this academic burlesque.

The Fiend lost his cool.
He freaked out and he snapped.
He said he was innocent.
His king had been trapped!

My teacher and The Fiend
were once symbiotic.
The bond is now broken.
Now it's purely chaotic!

The principal was called
to remove The Fiend.
No learning was happening,
so the principal intervened.

My teacher got busted
for concealing her phone.
The principal wasn't happy.
That's something she doesn't condone.

The Fiend was restrained
and escorted to the door.
He won a lot of battles,
but I had just won the war.

The teacher and The Fiend
were once thick as thieves.
A fairy-tale ending
to a story no one believes.

As The Fiend left the room
around 11:38.
I looked him in the eye
and whispered, "Checkmate."

I'm quiet and shy,
and now I sit alone.
That is my story of...
How to kill two birds with one phone.

WHERE EAGLES DARE

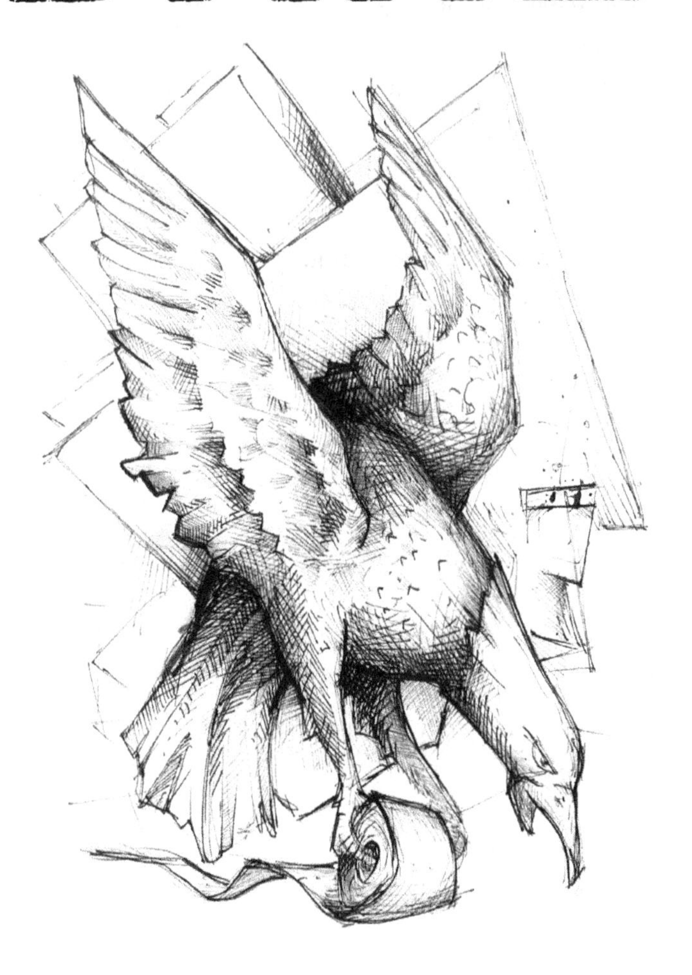

Every class that I have,
I sit in the front row.
Teachers say there's a reason.
I pretend I don't know.

I don't really agree,
but it's not up for debate.
There's a target on my back.
The front row is my fate.

I was paying attention
as anyone could see.
Suddenly it occurred to me,
I have to go pee.

I raised my hand,
but the teacher kept teaching.
She was rambling and babbling.
My eyes are beseeching.

My teacher is evil.
She won't look in my direction.
I'm going to send her the bill
for my bladder infection!

I tried to stay focused,
but it was really no use.
If I'm not mistaken,
isn't this child abuse?

My hand was still up,
which she chose to ignore.
So I blurted out...
"I CAN'T HOLD IT NO MORE!"

My teacher was annoyed.
She breathed a deep sigh.
She said, "Put your hand down.
We go at 10:55!"

"I can't wait any longer.
I'm begging you please."
She rolled her eyes and said, "FINE!"
I really hope I don't sneeze!

So I...

Ran out the door.
Sprinted down the hall.
I was doing *the dance*
straight to the bathroom stall.

Wait...WHAT?

The stall is empty.
Someone locked the door?
I hope their shots are up to date.
They had to crawl out on the floor!

I don't think it's a secret
what the boys' bathroom is like.
You almost need a hazmat suit.
Are students allowed to go on strike?

I prefer my privacy,
but the urinal will have to do.
Beggars can't be choosers.
At least I don't have to poo.

With a quick zip
I looked around, then down.
There's something in the urinal?
That something is brown!

Are my eyes deceiving me?
There's been a mistake.
I looked once again...
It's NOT a urinal cake!

Now I am horrified.
This is such a disgrace!
An eagle has landed
but in the wrong place!

I went back to my class,
and I told my teacher.
Her eyes were wide open
like she had just seen a creature!

She seemed in a panic.
She was in total disbelief.
Mr. C happened to walk by.
She breathed a sigh of relief.

She pulled him aside.
She filled him in.
He said, "You gotta be kidding!"
He started to grin.

I went back to the bathroom.
I showed Mr. C.
He started to laugh and said,
"I bet that wasn't easy!"

"Don't be offended,
I have to ask if it was you?"
"Nope ... I have to go number one,
not number two."

Mr. C just smiled.
We wrapped up our chitchat.
He looked once again and said,
"You really can't unsee that!"

I went back to my classroom,
confused and carefree.
It was right at that moment I realized...

I forgot to pee!

The very next day
I'm sitting in reading.
The teacher announced
that the boys have a meeting.

Color me curious,
I asked what it's about.
"Mr. C will tell you,
AND QUIT BLURTING OUT!"

Just then at our door
appeared Mr. C.
"Boys, please line up.
You are all coming with me."

Mr. C was confused.
He clearly wasn't happy.
He usually loves his job.
Today his job was crappy.

We headed to the bathroom,
to the scene of the crime.
They're taking this matter seriously.
It's not our assigned time?!

We entered the bathroom
where we all filed in.
And this is where the story
should actually begin.

"This is a urinal.
This is where you pee.
You do NOT poop here!
Do you understand me?"

We're all in agreement.
We now know where to pee.
We've cleared the air ... *so to speak.*
Mr. C seems a little grumpy?

Let's move on to the toilet,
a modern commode.
We'll get our ducks in a row
in this fork in the road.

"Now here is the deal.
This is the scoop.
The TOILET is the ONLY place
that you are supposed to go poop."

Mr. C asked all of us,
"Do you now understand?"
I think we all now know
where the eagle must land!

We've crossed a bridge.
No one ever confessed.
We all lined up and waited our turn
to put this new information to the test.

THE SNOWBALL EFFECT

Today after school
I made an executive decision.
I'm not doing my homework
because of a sneaking suspicion.

I heard some teachers talking
about the biggest blizzard in years.
They think school will be closing.
That's music to my ears!

Tomorrow's a big test
that has been causing me stress.
I haven't studied that much,
actually a little bit less.

Normally when I get home,
homework is supposed to come first.
But since school will be closing,
that decision's been reversed!

I made myself a snack,
got comfortable on the floor.
It's time to kick back
and play games on my Playstation 4.

My mom *may* not understand.
She'll probably think I'm lazy.
Mom's SERIOUS about school!
She's also bat-crap crazy!!

My mom came home
at 5:37.
"IS YOUR HOMEWORK DONE?"
She's loud ... she goes to eleven!

"Mom, there's a blizzard developing,
and it's heading our way.
School's will be closed
at least until Friday."

"THAT DOESN'T MATTER!
YOU KNOW THE HOUSE RULE!
HOMEWORK COMES FIRST
SO YOU ARE READY FOR SCHOOL!"

When it comes to homework,
my mom isn't playin'.
"GET YOUR BUTT IN THE KITCHEN!"
See what I'm sayin'?

I told her I'm finishing my game.
I want to beat my high score.
Turns out that was the WRONG answer,
an answer I'd deplore!

"I'M GOING TO COUNT TO THREE!
AND I'M STARTING AT TWO!!
YOU'LL GET YOUR BUTT IN THE KITCHEN!!!
IF YOU KNOW WHAT'S GOOD FOR YOU!!!!"

What happened after that
is still a little hazy.
My mom is off her rocker.
See what I mean ... bat-crap crazy!

I grabbed all of my books
and went to the kitchen.
My mom was mean mugging me.
My mom was still ... *well, you know!*

I did all of my homework
because my mom has a short fuse.
School should be canceled.
They'll announce it on the news.

The weather guy confirmed
what I heard this afternoon.
This blizzard could be huge.
I'll be sleeping 'til noon!

No decision was made,
but it's windy and snowing.
Even if school is still open,
there is NO WAY that I'm going!

Early the next morning—
my mom is so cruel—
she woke me up EXTRA early.
She said, **"GET READY FOR SCHOOL!"**

She's got to be kidding.
There must be a mistake.
There's a blizzard outside.
I think I have a stomachache!

She said a statement was released,
just announced on channel 8.
The bus routes have been cleared.
Well, isn't that just great!

The weatherman said *BE CAREFUL.*
The roads are really slick!
I hate our superintendent.
He deserves a swift kick!

This is really stupid.
I'm staying at home.
I'm going back to sleep.
"Mom, get out and leave me alone..."

On the ride to school
I learned I was grounded.
I’m just a rat in a cage.
My mom's rage is unfounded!

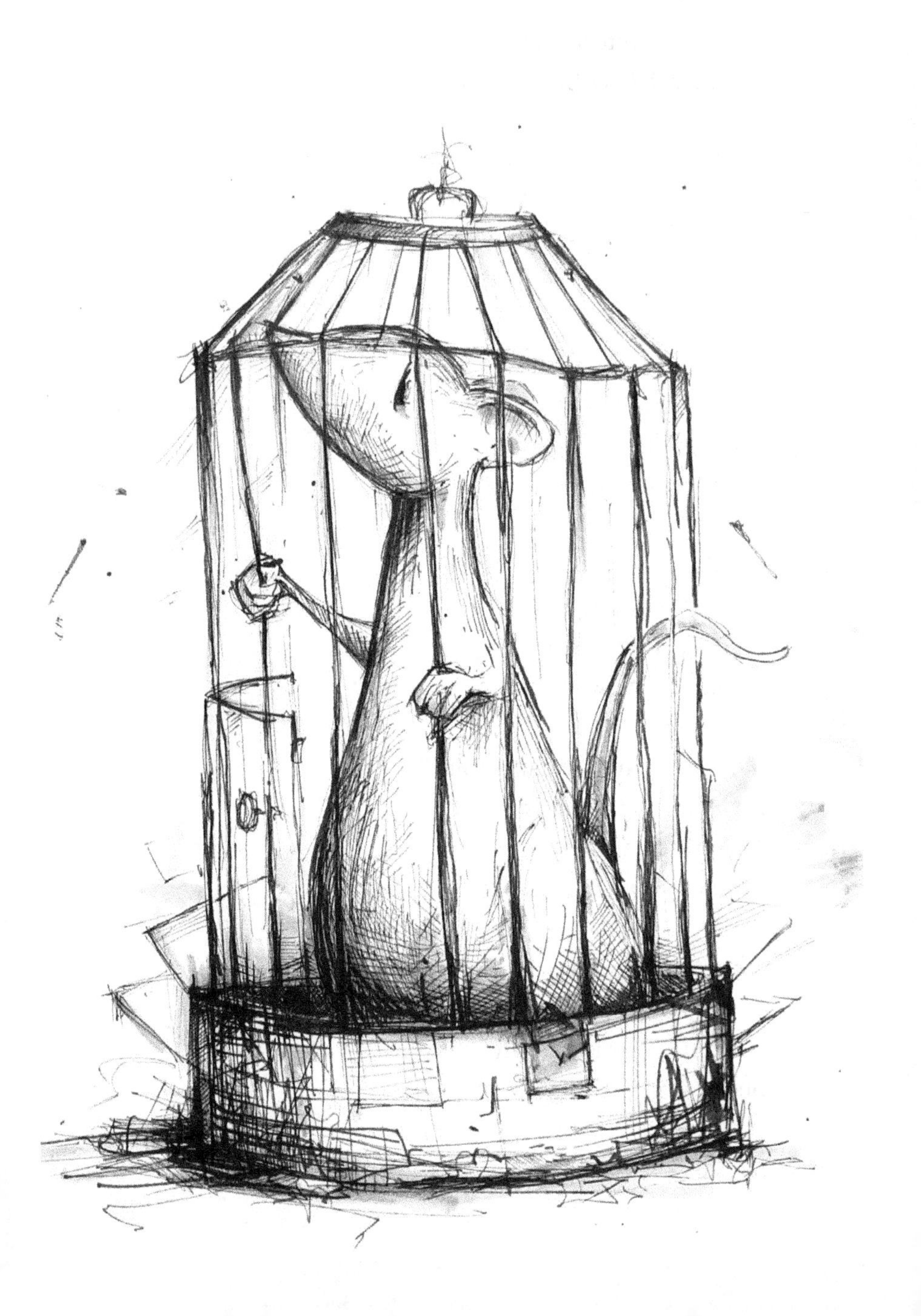

We left extra early,
which wasn't up for debate.
The roads were an ice rink.
AT LEAST I WASN'T LATE!

My friends all stayed home.
Their parents are cooler than mine.
They sent me Snapchats
playing video games online.

To rub salt on a wound
Mr. C canceled our exam.
I studied for no reason.
That's academic flimflam!

Wait ... we have a field trip?
How could I forget?
Mr. C said we're still going,
which I think we're going to regret!

"The roads are too dangerous."
Mr. C was raising a fuss.
The principal said quite sternly,
"You'll be fine ... get the kids on the bus."

He grudgingly did what she said,
but Mr. C was annoyed.
He said, "This is not safe!"
but he wants to stay employed.

Our bus made it three blocks
before we crashed into a tree.
We slid into someone's yard.
Mr. C was NOT happy!

We unloaded the bus
and walked back to school.
I just had on my hoodie.
This is so not cool!

Back in the classroom,
I was too cold to function.
Mr. C began teaching
Math-Targeted Instruction.

Something weird happened.
A student ran outside.
He yelled, "MATH IS STUPID!"
I laughed so hard that I cried!

This isn't unusual.
He does this stuff a lot.
There's a blizzard outside.
I think he forgot?

Mr. C watched him go,
then he started to laugh.
"He's not wearing a coat.
I'm betting he'll be back!"

Mr. C stopped teaching.
We watched out the window.
You're not going to believe this...
He started to disco!

Mr. C called the office,
and he told them the news.
Then out of the blue,
the kid took off his shoes!

There's a blizzard outside.
He's got to be freezing!
He just made a snow angel.
That is very misleading!

The principal came out and said,
"THIS FOOLISHNESS STOPS NOW!"
I don't think he agreed.
He called her a cow!

He tried making a snowball,
but the snow was too fluffy.
So he threw his socks at her.
He is really, REALLY huffy!

No shoes, no socks,
not even a coat.
When it comes to being naughty,
this kid is the GOAT!

I think the principal got cold
because she went back inside.
We've reached the eleventh hour.
Now it's about pride.

He outlasted the principal,
now he's throwing in the towel.
He's coming back to our room
using language that is foul!

Mr. C walked to the door.
He made sure it was locked?
He said we need to get back to work,
leaving all of us shocked!

"OPEN THE BLANKETY-BLANK DOOR!"
He was cold and shaking.
Mr. C said, "Go to the office.
The principal is waiting."

I can't unhear the words that were said
or unsee the gestures on display.
The student didn't shut the front door.
This has NOT been a very good day!

He finally succumbed
to being cold and exposed.
I shouldn't have to say this again, BUT...
"SCHOOL SHOULD HAVE BEEN CLOSED!"

MARVELOUS MERCHISTON

A REALLY long time ago,
there was a guy named John Napier.
Some believed he was a sorcerer.
For some, he elicited fear.

Rumors were rampant
about his connections to the occult.
Concerns of black magic.
Creating fear was the result.

He got mad at some pigeons,
so he put a spell on the flock—
you heard that correctly—
leaving his neighbor in shock.

To add fuel to the fire,
rumors of a black rooster that talks.
He traveled with a black spider.
He kept it in a small box.

He looked at the world differently.
He was a thinker outside the box.
It had nothing to do with that spider.
Don't cross him ... Napier's sly as a fox!

The Marvelous Merchiston
was not a magician.
He was a physicist, an astronomer,
most notably ... a mathematician.

He wasn't a sorcerer.
He didn't dabble in the macabre.
There was no black magic.
He invented a thingamabob.

He designed futuristic weapons
that could cause chaos and terror.
Napier destroyed all the plans,
knowing he'd made an error!

He invented logarithms
and created Napier's Bones.
Logarithms can measure earthquakes,
though there are still some unknowns.

He improved the lattice method,
making multiplying easier.
What student wouldn't like that?
You can thank John Napier!

His infamous black rooster
was a normal rooster painted black.
He did it to catch a thief
and to get his stuff back.

Tools were being stolen
from a shed where they were kept.
He lined up all the suspects,
knowing they were slightly inept.

He told them what happens
when you pet his psychic rooster.
The black rooster would crow,
identifying the shifty booster.

Each suspect entered a blackened room
and was told to pet the clairvoyant bird.
The thief's identity would be revealed.
Think about it ... it's not that absurd.

When each of them came out,
their hands were covered in black paint,
except for one suspect
who chose deceitful restraint.

He didn't pet the rooster,
fearing being reprimanded.
Having a guilty conscience
caught this thief *red-handed.*

An irritating neighbor
can really REALLY suck!
It's like they do stuff on purpose,
which makes them a total schmuck!

Napier's neighbor had pigeons
that ate up all of his grain.
He was constantly shooing them off.
It was driving him insane.

Napier confronted his neighbor,
giving him a piece of his mind.
His neighbor just laughed in his face.
The conversation quickly declined!

Well, that was not smart.
He just irritated him more.
Napier came up with a plan.
He would soon even the score.

He scattered peas throughout his field,
knowing the pigeons would persist.
He soaked the peas in alcohol,
knowing the pigeons couldn't resist.

Just like Napier predicted,
the pigeons all came back.
They ate up all the peas.
It's time for a little payback.

The pigeons were unable to fly.
His actions were calculated.
Napier put the pigeons in a bag.
The birds were inebriated!

It wasn't a demonic spell,
which is what his neighbor believed.
The birds were three sheets to the wind.
Napier's goal had been achieved.

Napier outsmarted his neighbor,
causing him to raise a white flag.
One thing I'm still curious about...
What do you do with drunk pigeons in a bag?

DARK SIDE OF THE WALL

It's just after lunch,
I'm sitting in science.
I sit by myself,
something about compliance.

The class settled down
as we eventually do.
It came to my attention
I need to go number two.

Here is the problem.
I have this strict rule.
That is just something
I will NOT do at school.

Say what you will,
you can laugh all you want.
Kids can be jerks!
They love to taunt!

If you don't understand,
just think for a minute.
Wet floors, the sounds, the smells...
That's pushing my limit!

I'll have to break my rule.
I don't want to conform.
These are uncharted waters.
It's always calm before the storm.

I raised my hand
so I can dismiss.
I'd rather swim with sharks
or fall into the abyss!

Wait just a minute?
There's a stench in the air?
That didn't come from me!
This totally isn't fair!

I put my hand down
because I can't go now.
Everyone will blame me.
That I just can't allow!

The teacher stopped teaching.
We all covered our noses.
It was silent but deadly.
This is no bed of roses!

Our windows don't open,
which I've never understood.
The teacher sprayed Febreeze.
It still doesn't smell good!

I am stuck in between
a rock and a hard place.
I REALLY gotta go NOW!
BUT ... I want to save face!

Just then I had an idea.
I rudely blurted out...
$^&*#%^!*$ &* %@$***^#!!
I got myself kicked out!

My teacher was mad.
My mom will be madder.
I'll deal with that later.
I have a more pressing matter.

I ran out the door.
I ran down the hall.
I ran straight to the office... *Just kidding.*
I ran straight to the bathroom stall.

With not a minute to spare,
I was in a big rush.
The stall was open.
SOMEONE FORGOT TO FLUSH!

I don't like this at all.
This is as good as it will get.
This is freaking me out!
"WHY IS THE SEAT WET!?"

So I'm looking around
and feeling rebellious.
There's a lot of graffiti.
Who is this Elvis?

I'm kind of surprised
how much writing there is.
Pictures and misspellings.
There's even a quiz.

Most of it's naughty,
which isn't surprising at all.
Then something got my attention
that was more than just scrawl.

Most of the graffiti was written
with a pen in black ink,
except for one word that was brown.
And WOW did it stink!

I know what you're thinking.
I should not have broken my rule.
This is a perfect example...
WHY I DON'T DO THIS AT SCHOOL!

I ran to the office
after I finished my business.
The principal was waiting.
She's mad ... I may need a witness.

"WHERE HAVE YOU BEEN?
WHAT WERE YOU THINKING?
I'M CALLING YOUR MOM!
WE'RE HAVING A MEETING!"

I was dazed and confused
from what I just saw.
The principal was yelling
about a camel and some straw?

"HAVE YOU LOST YOUR MIND?
THAT LANGUAGE IS NOT OK!
I KNOW YOU KNOW BETTER!
YOU'RE SUSPENDED AS OF TODAY!"

"Wait just a minute.
Please let me explain.
I just saw something
that's hard to ascertain."

I told her the story.
I don't think she believes it.
I raised a red flag.
Does she think I'm the culprit?

I re-explained my problem.
She's unsympathetic.
She doesn't believe me.
My story is problematic?

"I KNOW YOU THINK YOU'RE FUNNY.
YOU LIKE BEING THE CLASS CLOWN.
YOU'VE GOT ANOTHER THING COMING!
THIS TIME YOU'RE GOING DOWN!!"

"Come see for yourself.
I'm telling you the truth.
What's smeared on the wall
is NOT a Baby Ruth!"

We went back to the bathroom,
to the scene of the crime.
I'm NEVER coming back here!
This will be the last time!

The evidence was still there.
Like where would it go?
The principal saw firsthand
the restroom horror show.

She couldn't believe her eyes
at what she was seeing.
"THIS BATHROOM IS DISGUSTING!"
I bet there'll be a meeting.

ELVIS
WAS
HERE

We went back to the office.
She called in Mr. C.
I was dismissed to the hall.
I wonder if he's still mad at me?

The very next day
at the beginning of school,
I didn't get suspended?
IKR ... that was totally cool!

The rumors were flying
about the bathroom wall.
The girls called us gross.
They made fun of us in the hall.

They teased us and mocked us.
They used words that were obscene.
I guess I can't blame them.
That bathroom was like a crime scene!

As rumors usually do,
they snowballed for weeks.
The girls were relentless
with their comments and mean tweets...

#notabrowncrayon
#elvisdidnotdoit
#soapisyourfriend
#cannoteatababyruthcandybareveragain

We made it to Friday.
It's been another long week.
I was floating without a paddle
up a certain smelly creek!

The custodian walked in
looking rather disgusted.
He said it has happened again.
None of us can be trusted!

The girls erupted in laughter.
Their teasing was excess.
The girls were dismissed.
THEY GOT TO GO TO RECESS!

The custodian was mad.
This was causing him stress.
"Someone has to know something.
SOMEONE NEEDS TO CONFESS!"

Well, that didn't happen
as you'd probably expect.
While the girls were enjoying recess,
we had to talk about respect.

This totally isn't fair.
The boys have been branded.
Bathrooms are now closely monitored
because an eagle crash-landed.

Not lost in this story
there's someone among us.
They're going for a hat trick.
They need thrown under the bus!

The truth was discovered.
A suspect had been caught.
It was just a matter of time...
This story grossed me out a lot!

As simple as that,
the mystery was solved.
The girls should've listened to me.
I TOLD THEM I WASN'T INVOLVED!

A weight has been lifted.
This experience has ended.
But the girls are still taunting us.
I'm a little offended!

We've been exonerated.
The girls wouldn't let it go.
It's been a long couple of weeks
with this dog-and-pony show.

The escapades were over.
Several weeks had passed.
Things got back to normal,
but normal wouldn't last.

The custodian stopped by,
which he hadn't done in a while.
He didn't look angry,
but I didn't see him smile.

He was talking to Mr. C.
We were definitely curious.
It's right before recess.
SERIOUSLY ... I WILL BE FURIOUS!

The class was stirring.
We can't hear what they're saying.
I know where this is going.
The girls will be preying!

I think I just heard a word
I know I shouldn't repeat.
But then Mr. C said...
"Boys, go to recess. Girls ... stay in your seat."

YOU HEARD THAT CORRECTLY.
THE GIRLS JUST TOOK ONE ON THE CHIN.
THE BOYS ARE HEADING TO RECESS.
THAT'S A HAT TRICK FOR THE WIN!

As God is my witness,
this story is true.
Elvis has left the building,
and now this story is through.

Seriously ... who is Elvis?

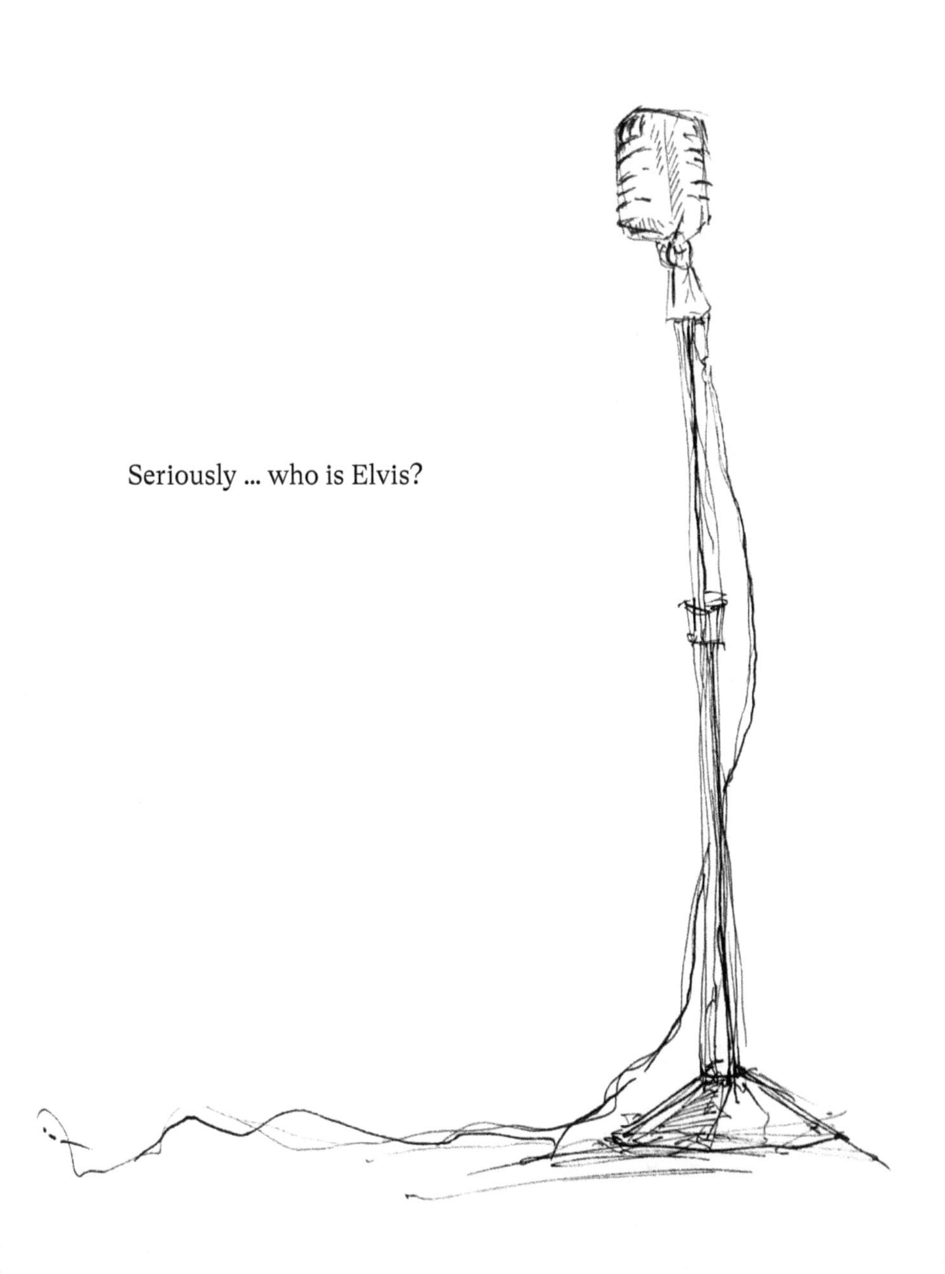

HOW WAS YOUR DAY?

When a parent asks the question,
How was your day?
Here's a quick tip:
Be CAREFUL what you say!

The question seems harmless,
very innocent at first.
It's all smoke and mirrors.
You're being coerced!

Parents are curious
and very persistent.
They want in your business.
They're very insistent!

When the question arises,
and I promise it will,
just say the following
so your parents will chill.

"Great! Thank you for asking.
How was your day?"
You closed that door
and kept the wolves at bay.

You're not out of the woods yet.
Beware of the question that comes next.
Skeletons are listening.
It might leave you perplexed!

"Has anything happened
that you might like to share?"
That question is loaded.
THAT QUESTION ISN'T FAIR!

They say it with a tone
that you did not expect.
The look on their face
makes them shady and suspect.

You just stepped in something.
How long have they known?
Did they talk to my teacher?
Did something just moan?

You cannot remember
doing anything wrong.
Your mind is racing.
This was a setup all along!

This trick is effective
to get you to confess.
They're playing devil's advocate.
Don't expect anything less.

Look in your closet
through the sticks and the stones.
If you're caught in a lie,
you can blame it on the bones!

TWO FINGERS FOR YOU

When I am sitting in school
time seems to stand still.
Today was even slower,
I forgot to take my pill.

Friday has arrived
the third best day of the week.
It's a day I've never missed,
you can call it a streak.

See ... if I'm absent on Friday,
then my weekend is shot.
No phone or friends are allowed.
Trust me ... it stinks a lot!

I've done my due diligence
all of my work is turned in.
I'd be grounded if I didn't.
In our house that's a sin!

So when the gates of hell open
at precisely 2:54,
the gatekeeper yells, "SLOW DOWN!"
I'm the first one out the door.

Another week in the books
as I bid a happy adieu.
It's not that I hate school.
Who am I kidding ... yes I do!

I didn't always feel this way.
I can't pinpoint when it changed.
It's a hooligan's holiday
in a school for the deranged!

A girl in my history class,
she thinks she's a cat.
She hisses and meows...
What's up with that!

A guy in biology,
he's always wearing a cape.
He is NOT a superhero
or Severus Snape.

Two students in English
I call Thing One and Thing Two.
They constantly cause problems.
There's nothing the teacher can do.

Please tell me this isn't normal,
that I'm not losing my mind.
Teachers don't say anything.
The blind leading the blind.

The inmates are in charge
with excuses galore.
They're running the asylum
doing stuff teachers abhor!

Now for the business at hand,
which does NOT involve learning.
I'm going to Snapchat with my friends.
Some ears will be burning.

I'm hanging outside
chill'n in my front yard.
No cats, no capes, no *things* allowed.
Just call me avant-garde.

I've got my soccer ball.
I'm working on a new trick.
I'll post it to my story.
My friends will think it's sick!

I hope this one girl
will see it on my post.
Every time I try to talk to her,
I feel like I've seen a ghost.

I always get nervous
when I see her around.
I'd like to reach for the stars,
but my feet won't leave the ground.

Unbeknownst to me,
my world was about to change.
Some kid I've never seen walked by.
He was the definition of strange.

For whatever reason,
he won't stop staring at me.
It's really REALLY awkward!
Apparently, there's a *thing three.*

I was doing my own thing,
not bothering a soul,
when this Mean Thing Three
laughs at me and calls me an @#$*^%#!

I have no clue why this happened,
but he got under my skin.
It's an eye for an eye
with my feelings of chagrin.

This is a situation
where it's best to think before you speak.
That did NOT cross my mind...
I said shut up and called him a freak!

I knew right when I said it,
I wish I'd kept my mouth shut.
Buuuut ... that wasn't the case.
He proceeded to kick my butt!

He cracked the screen on my phone,
kicked my soccer ball down the street.
I got whooped in my own front yard,
which he promised to repeat!

I’m not making excuses,
but he was nearly twice my size.
I’m pretty sure Mean Thing Three
is the devil in disguise!

If you think I should tell someone,
then you are insane!
That would FOR SURE make things worse,
bringing more violence and pain!

Mean Thing Three is a thug!
I just want this to be through.
I'm going to keep my mouth shut!
I'll lie if I have to.

Parents and teachers mean well,
they really truly do.
Kids have their own code of conduct
parents and teachers can't construe.

I retrieved my soccer ball.
He scuffed it all up.
I really need to learn
to keep my mouth shut!

My iPhone screen is cracked,
which I can't afford to fix.
To ward off Mean Thing Three,
I'm getting a crucifix!

My level of concern
has now gone through the roof.
Where did this jerk come from?
I'd like to make him go POOF!

I went inside my house
and put some ice on my face.
My face and ego were bruised.
The jerk put me in my place!

I need to come up with a story
to explain the day's events.
A story that won't seem suspicious
or warrant my parents' two cents.

As I sat on the couch pondering,
my dog jumped up on my lap.
Animals have a sixth sense.
She curled up and took a nap.

My dog is so awesome.
She takes good care of me.
Rosie likes to cuddle and bark.
She wouldn't hurt a flea.

When my parents got home,
they were taken aback.
The questions were flying,
but I never did crack.

I made up a story
that wasn't complex.
I did what I had to do,
with fingers crossed ... King's X.

I told them I had an accident
playing football in P.E.
The nurse said I'd be fine.
Avoiding eye contact was key.

I don't think they bought it.
I know they're suspicious.
For now, I dodged a bullet
with my story that's fictitious.

If I spill all the beans,
my mom will go ballistic!
Trust me. I've seen it happen!
I'm not being pessimistic.

I fear being taunted and teased
over this unexpected strife.
I fear being beaten
within an inch of my life!

If I stick to my story,
then I'll be living in fear.
If I get caught in a lie...
I may as well disappear!

All cards on the table,
I feel guilty for lying.
It's a catch-22.
My options are horrifying!

Over the next several days
I felt dazed and confused.
I was scared of my own shadow.
Mean Thing Three would be amused.

I kept looking over my shoulder
for something that wasn't there.
I was a deer in headlights.
Sometimes life isn't fair!

I avoided the front yard
for reasons crystal clear.
I stayed inside my house.
I hate living in fear!

Playing with my dog, Rosie,
is where I found solace.
If Mean Thing Three returns,
his victory would be flawless!

I just have this feeling
that our paths are gonna cross.
I hate Mean Thing Three!
He's a foreboding albatross!

I know there are bullies
and sometimes people are mean.
I'm at the end of my rope!
Maybe I should just come clean?

No one's been over lately.
I've been keeping to myself.
I hang out with my dog, Rosie.
My social life is on the shelf.

Today, out of the blue,
my best friend stopped by.
I made him quickly come inside,
which made him ask, "Why?"

Usually when he comes over,
we shoot hoops in my driveway.
We play one-on-one and talk trash.
It's mostly just horseplay.

I told him the story
about how I got beat up.
He laughed and made fun of me...
I told him to shut up!

He's rubbing Rosie's belly
while they're sitting on the floor.
My best friend loves my dog.
Those two have a good rapport.

He said he was just kidding—
he can break this stranglehold.
"The answer is under your nose
to be avenged sevenfold."

When he made that statement,
he wore a devilish grin.
I know the grass is always greener
where the dogs are fenced in.

My best friend is awesome,
but he likes to push the envelope.
I know I've dug a deep hole
while walking a tightrope.

"You need to make a point
to be in your front yard.
Keep Rosie outside with you
to even the scorecard."

It was just at that moment
that the stars all aligned.
Rosie was the answer
to give me peace of mind.

Rosie is a sweetheart,
as I'm sure you're believing.
Mean Thing Three doesn't know this.
Looks can be deceiving.

The glass is now half full.
Rosie is the clincher.
Did I happen to mention...

Rosie is a Doberman pinscher.

The idea was quite simple.
I game planned with my friend.
Rosie was my ace in the hole,
my means to an end.

My best friend and I
will be playing one-on-one.
Rosie will be in the garage,
awaiting her day in the sun.

With home field advantage
and a plan that's audacious,
Mean Thing Three's future
is about to get hellacious!

I want him to fear for his life!
Rosie is an intimidating sight.
She's a hundred pounds of muscle!
But her bark is worse than her bite.

He needs to learn a lesson.
You shouldn't pick on a stranger.
There are consequences for your actions.
Rosie is a game changer!

Justice is coming.
Rosie will keep me protected.
Live by the sword, die by the sword.
Expect the unexpected!

For the next several days,
we were lying in wait.
No sign of Mean Thing Three.
He's probably an inmate!

I was nervous and excited
to launch our barrage.
Words will be flying.
Rosie is in the garage.

Days turned to weeks,
and we started to lose hope.
Maybe it's for the better
to avoid this slippery slope.

I'd almost given up
when *you know who* appeared.
For some strange reason,
all my fear disappeared.

At first he didn't see me.
I knew just what to do.
I yelled, "Hey $&*%@$$...
I have two fingers for you!"

I caught him off guard
by what I had just said.
You know his blood was boiling.
I had him seeing red!

@#$ %$^&*#$% %^&*(*)%$#@@!
%$#^@!&**!!!***&***!!
@#$ %$^&*#$% %^&*(*%$#@@!!!
$#@#%^**/+^%$#@##%^$$...!!!!

I'm not going to translate that
because NONE of it is nice.
The gist is ... he beat me up once,
and he would like to do it twice!

It's time for Mean Thing Three
to be sent into a tailspin.
I hope you're sitting down.
Let the games begin!

I called him more names,
baiting him into my yard.
I'm gonna take down the bad guy
like John McClane in Die Hard.

His fists were clenched.
He made a beeline for me.
I gave him the peace sign,
then I hollered for Rosie.

Right on command,
Rosie came and sat by my side.
She was wiggling and barking.
My actions are justified!

Rosie has been trained.
She is very obedient.
What Mean Thing Three doesn't know,
that's my secret ingredient!

He stopped dead in his tracks
when he saw Rosie appear.
I think someone walked over his grave.
Mean Thing Three couldn't hide his fear.

If there's a light in the attic,
his barely turns on.
He knows where the sidewalk ends.
He's not coming onto my lawn!

He was getting ready to run.
Getting beat up hurt my pride.
I just couldn't help myself,
I said something a little snide.

"Roses are red
and violets are blue.
Rosie is going to bite someone
I'll give you three guesses who..."

He took off like lightning.
I yelled, "Never come back, capisce?"
Suddenly my plan hit a snag.
Rosie got off her leash!

All hell had broken loose!
So much for the afterglow.
I'm not sure what Rosie will do.
To quote Scooby Doo, "Ruh-roh!"

One thing leads to another.
Rosie loves to play chase.
If you take off running,
she'll catch you and lick your face.

Rosie LOVES to rough house,
and she's really REALLY fast!
She knocked Mean Thing Three to the ground.
He thought today would be his last!!

Mean Thing Three screamed for his life.
It was a sound of pure terror.
Maybe I should've thought this through.
This may have been an error.

I hollered for Rosie.
I was completely ignored.
As I said once before...
Live by the sword, die by the sword!

Rosie was on top of him
like white on rice.
Mean Thing Three screamed, "I'M SORRY!"
Not once, but twice!

My mom came outside
when she heard the commotion.
She assessed the situation.
I think she had a notion.

My mom gave me a hard look,
which I know what that'll mean.
I'm going to be on house arrest.
I'm going to have to come clean.

My best friend in the world
tried to run for the hills.
My mom stopped him dead in his tracks.
Her stare can give you the chills!

She whistled for Rosie,
a loud two-syllable trill.
I don't know how she does that.
I think I may need a will!

Rosie's ears perked up
when she heard my mom's command.
I guess I have to admit,
things got a little out of hand.

Rosie came running
'cause she knows she'll get a treat.
Rosie gave him one last lick.
Mean Thing Three had tasted defeat!

Clearly he was shaken.
Mean Thing Three tried to walk away.
My mom wasn't having that.
She said, "You're going to stay!"

It was time to come clean.
I told my mom the whole truth.
I was hoping for leniency.
Can you blame it on my youth?

She made ME apologize
for scaring Mean Thing Three!
I'm the one that got beat up!
And I'M getting the third degree?!

My mom is the judge and jury.
I don't think I got a fair trial.
I'M THE ONE THAT GOT BEAT UP!
I'm declaring a mistrial!

Even my best friend
had to apologize for his role.
It came from the back of his hand.
He got thirty days in the hole!

Mean Thing Three was gloating
while we got put in our place.
I told him things that Rosie licks...
Now that's all over his face!

My goal was accomplished,
but it came with a price.
Mean Thing Three now knows
Rosie is actually nice.

Suddenly my confidence
turned back into fear.
I don't want to get beat up again.
Mean Thing Three started to jeer.

My mom turned her attention,
and she addressed Mean Thing Three.
He lied through his teeth,
blaming everything on me!

My mom then APOLOGIZED
for the events that have occured.
"There WON'T be anymore problems,
you can be rest assured."

As she talked to Mean Thing Three,
I knew he had only one thought.
He wants me pushing up daisies.
This wasn't over by a long shot.

Mean Thing Three got snarky.
He feels he has the upper hand.
He talked smack to my mom!
We are now in no-man's-land!!

My best friend and I
would love to disappear.
Mean Thing Three must have a death wish.
He is showing no fear!

My mom wasn't fazed
by his cursing that was cliché.
As Mean Thing Three was leaving,
my mom said, "Oh by the way..."

She said something in German
that I've never heard her say.
Rosie started barking and growling.
It was a vicious display!

"Rosie is obedient.
She does exactly what I say.
I know EVERYTHING that's happened.
It's time for you to go away!"

"I think you get the picture
how things can go down.
Rosie's bark is worse than her bite...
Or is it the other way around?"

Nothing more needed to be said.
The message was clear.
Mean Thing Three was scared straight.
Now HE had something to fear!

LIe
CHeaT
STeaL

Folklore and fairytales
and even Dr. Seuss
say three is a magical number.
Beetlejuice, Beetlejuice, **STOP!**

Three little pigs.
The three musketeers.
Hear, see, and speak no evil.
Things aren't always as it appears.

Three wishes, three challenges.
Three strikes and you're out.
Even three blind mice
will see what it's about.

Let's go out on a limb
for a view that's profound.
Three sides to every story.
What goes around comes around.

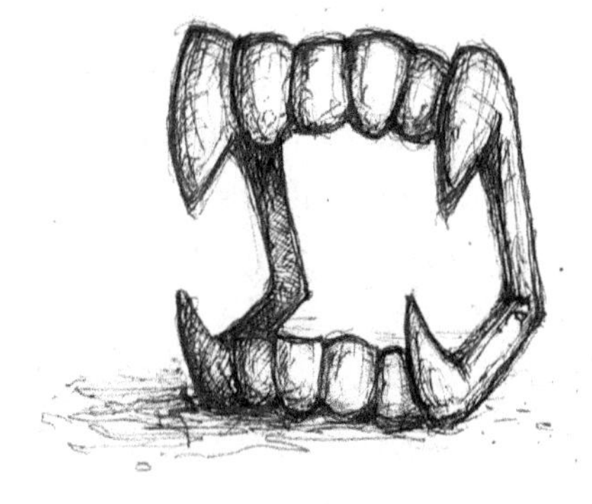

Mr. C was teaching
when he gave a student *the look.*
The student wasn't listening.
He was doodling on his notebook.

This wasn't uncommon.
He's often off task.
He doesn't cause problems.
He wears his hoodie like a mask.

Mr. C didn't yell.
He didn't freak out.
He asked matter-of-factly,
"What's this all about?"

He had artistically sketched
the words *lie, cheat, and steal.*
He said he heard it on *The Simpsons.*
"It's not a big deal."

"Can I tell you a story
'bout the words you have written?
I'll tell it next Friday.
But until then ... you have to listen."

Not knowing what to think,
he nervously agreed.
A horticulturist
had just planted a seed.

True to his word,
he was focused and alert.
He even kept his hoodie down
as the teacher would assert.

So when Friday arrived,
it was the first thing he'd ask.
It's time to pay up.
He was focused and on task.

Just as was promised,
we were given a story.
Some parts were venomous
and far from obligatory.

The stories he told,
he says they are accredited.
But some parts are too explicit...
so some parts have been edited!

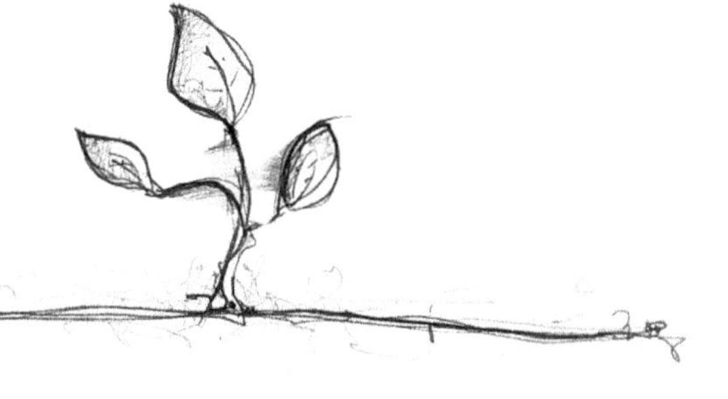

LIE

One day after school
a former student came to visit.
She was all in a rage.
Her language was explicit!

She had been kicked out of class
and in school suspended.
She threw shade at the teacher.
Apparently, he's easily offended.

"I hate being in his class!
It's like sitting in prison.
The teacher totally hates me!
Some problems have arisen."

Mr. C listened intently,
then offered a solution.
She wasn't going to like it,
but it was a resolution.

"Think about this teacher.
Math makes him happy.
Math makes you miserable.
Then you start actin' crappy."

"You became a distraction,
then you got removed.
Now you're in school suspended.
His day has just improved."

"If you keep fighting this battle,
I promise you'll lose.
Now you're on his radar
because you have a short fuse."

"I know what you can do
to survive the semester.
If you don't fix this problem now,
your problems will fester."

"Before the school day even starts,
you're going to pay him a visit.
You'll apologize and get extra help.
Your attitude will be exquisite!"

"I doubt he'll make it easy.
You've been nothing but a pain.
The teacher has nothing to lose,
and you have everything to gain."

**"ARE YOU OUT OF YOUR MIND?
I'M NOT GOING BACK TO HIS CLASS!
THE TEACHER TOTALLY HATES ME!
HE CAN KISS MY ... UUUGGGHHH!!!"**

"Well, that's where you're wrong.
Please do this for me.
Did I mention you're my favorite student?
And I asked very nicely?"

While she rolled her eyes,
she started to whine,
"That's totally not fair.
I won't do it ... **OK FINE!"**

A deal had been reached.
She thought Mr. C was mean.
She rolled her eyes.
Mr. C needed caffeine!

The next day after school,
she returned to see Mr. C.
He asked how it went.
She said, "That was NOT easy!"

"He was totally shocked
to see me at his door.
I apologized and asked for help.
His jaw nearly hit the floor!"

"I did everything you said.
I agree that it did work.
He let me back into his class,
but I still think he's a jerk!"

"Whether that's true or not,
you should be very proud!
Now do the same thing tomorrow..."

I just cursed out loud!

She said, "Absolutely not!
Once was enough!
I have no reason to go back.
I understand all of that stuff."

"You've taken the bull by the horns,
and I know that you get it.
You're on a road to redemption,
and you're building up credit."

"This feels like extortion.
This was your plan all the while.
This is above and beyond
going the extra mile!"

While she rolled her eyes,
she let out a scream.
"I CAN'T EVEN DEAL WITH YOU!
YOU'RE LIKE A BAD DREAM!"

Both sides had come to terms
though it was *slightly* one-sided.
"I don't feel like your favorite student.
I'm feeling misguided!"

The next day after school,
she went back to see Mr. C.
He asked how it went.
"Thanks to you, my stomach is queasy!"

"I went in early this morning.
I was tired and surly.
He met me at the door.
I hate getting up that early!"

"I told him ... I think that I get it,
but I want to make sure.
He looked like he saw a ghost.
For me it was torture!"

"I let him *re-explain*
things I already know.
I smiled and said thank you.
For the second day in a row."

Mr. C was so proud,
and he totally should be.
But I have a funny feeling
things are about to get ugly!

"I know that was hard,
but the teacher's coming around.
Please ... just one more time?
Your impact is profound!"

While she rolled her eyes,
she turned her back on Mr. C.
"THERE ISN'T A CHANCE I'LL GO BACK
AND YOU CAN'T MAKE ME!"

"Early the next morning,
about 7:03,
I was back asking for help...
Shut up ... don't judge me!"

"It must be cooling off
in that place that is hot.
He said he was happy to see me?
I'm scared ... he might be a robot!"

"I gathered my bearings
and completed my mission.
I got MORE extra help
on this misleading expedition."

"And now I'm sure that it's frozen
in that very scary hot place.
He said... "I wish more students were like you."
This teacher is from an alien race!"

A glutton for punishment
as you clearly have seen.
She went back to see Mr. C.
She can't believe he's so mean!

She told him about her expedition
over now frozen terrain.
The robot, an alien race.
Mr. C agreed her day was insane!

Mr. C wasn't surprised
by the temperature change.
He thought he should be wearing a coat,
but it's really not that strange.

She entered his world.
She showed the teacher respect.
Mr. C didn't want to brag,
but he did tell her he was correct!

"Don't you feel guilty
that you've taught me all these lies?"
Mr. C just laughed,
and then he rolled his eyes.

CHEAT

Teachers ... I'm not going to lie.
Some days it's hard to stay awake.
There is a girl in our class,
she easily takes the cake.

She's crashed out on her desk
before class even began.
I wouldn't try to wake her
because *something* will hit the fan!

Nobody will mess with her.
If you do, you'll start a feud!
She hangs out with two other girls.
The notorious ... LEGION OF 'TUDE!

They're always together.
Their atti-"tude" is huge!
If you cross any one of them,
I suggest seeking refuge!

They don't turn in assignments
or homework when it's collected.
Fighty-"tude" has been arrested.
Sassy-"tude" is connected.

Wreaking havoc throughout the day,
they are as bad as advertised!
But don't judge this book by its cover.
You'll be notoriously surprised.

At the end of school one day
when Sleepy-"tude" was awoke,
Mr. C said we need to talk.
She said this has got to be a joke!

She started to talk trash,
then knocked her books to the floor.
The class was dismissed.
The Legion laughing, heading out the door.

Mr. C is usually pretty chill,
but as we left ... he slammed the door shut.
And then we heard him yell...

“PICK THESE BOOKS UP!”

Nobody really knows
what happened behind that closed door.
It was suddenly eerily quiet.
Does Mr. C know he started a war?

The students were all curious,
but nobody dared to ask.
Talking about The Legion
would be too daunting of a task.

The next day at school
Sleepy-"tude" was nowhere we could see.
We assumed she got suspended
for throwing atti-"tude" at Mr. C.

A week had gone by
before Sleepy-"tude" reappeared.
Some things started to change,
but The Legion was still feared!

One thing most intriguing,
which you know made her furious.
Sleepy-"tude" was staying after school?
I'm not lying ... I'm totally serious!

It must be her punishment
for acting up and sleeping a lot.
Mr. C wasn't playing ... BUT,
this can't be over by a long shot!

Sassy-"tude" and Fighty-"tude"
started to slowly keep things in check.
They were loyal friends ... but
NOT when Mr. C's mad as heck!

So this story called "Cheat"
happened just like you have read.
But ... it's more like a confession.
You've been intentionally misled.

You may have mixed feelings.
You have been cheated from the truth.
Let's put this puzzle together.
It's time to become a sleuth.

Sleepy-"tude" cared about school.
She was really quite bright,
but where she comes from, that isn't cool.
It's more respected to know how to fight.

Mr. C had figured this out.
He devised a plan that was grand.
Their interactions became staged
like a magician's sleight of hand.

She had a spot in the office
when she was kicked out of class.
When you thought she was in trouble...
her grades were kicking *butt!*

The Legion was none the wiser,
with the "tude" she earned praise.
While she was in school suspended,
she was earning all As.

So how was that possible
when she never took her work home?
Mr. C secretly gave her books
and tutored her over the phone.

Sleeping through the lessons
was actually not fake.
She had family responsibilities
that she could not forsake.

Oh yeah ... I almost forgot...

When Mr. C slammed the door shut
and totally lost his cool?
It was all just part of the act.
He knew he was acting like a fool!

That's pretty much how things went.
Things aren't always as it appears.
Don't allow yourself to be cheated
by friends, teachers, parents, or peers.

STEAL

Being the new kid at school
is an interesting prospect.
A lot rides on first impressions.
You hope you get it correct.

Such was the case for a new girl,
an *outsider* to our school.
She burst into Mr. C's class yelling...
"I DON'T CARE, THAT'S A DUMB RULE!"

One of the teachers was absent,
the others were weathering the storm.
There were no subs available,
which was typically the norm.

Whenever that happens,
learning is less than great.
There are twenty-four students in that class.
Now they have thirty-eight.

She'd been here less than a week
before she got kicked out of her classroom.
A personality conflict?
That teacher is known for riding a broom.

Mr. C was at capacity.
Learning was an academic burlesque.
There was one seat open.
She went and sat at Mr. C's desk!

Curiosity killed the cat,
but we still watched what she would do.
Mr. C walked over to her and said,
"Please open your book to page 152."

Mr. C didn't want a battle.
He was just trying to survive.
The other class had thirty-eight students,
Mr. C had forty-five.

The New Girl had an edge,
a devil-may-care preview.
It's the coming attraction.
Evil will be getting its due!

She slammed open her book,
not likely to the correct page.
While sitting on a soft comfy chair,
something distracted her from her rage.

That something was not nothing.
That not nothing was something.
The New Girl would be blindsided
by something *evil* that's not nothing!

Sitting on Mr. C's desk
was a purple Tyrannosaurus rex,
better known as Barney the Dinosaur.
A kids' doll no one respects.

Barney ruled the '90s.
The theme song was contagious.
Idolized by millions of toddlers,
his popularity was outrageous!

Evil Barney was a gift
from a favorite former student.
Mr. C kept it on his desk.
But not purely for amusement.

Evil Barney came in handy
if a student would misbehave.
Evil Barney would sit on your desk.
A memory you'd take to your grave!

The taunting was relentless.
Kids would laugh and call you a freak.
If Evil Barney was stolen or harmed,
the class would lose recess for a week.

I know that sounds crazy,
a child's toy instilling fear.
But it works like a charm
when your classmates all jeer!

Barney wasn't always evil,
at least not when he started.
He went through a transformation
from annoying to evil wholehearted.

As to what makes Barney evil
besides making students feel precarious?
Mr. C gave him vampire teeth...
We thought it was hilarious!

The New Girl picked Evil Barney up.
Forty-five students went silent.
Nobody had the nerve to say a word.
Call it a gut feeling ... she could become violent!

Mr. C continued teaching,
his class busting at the seam.
He kept an eye on The New Girl.
A monkey wrench in the regime.

The New Girl calmed down,
though I wouldn't call her warm and snugly.
When her teacher came to get her...
That's when things got ugly!

Her teacher clearly wasn't happy.
I don't think The New Girl even cared.
She said she wasn't going anywhere.
The New Girl wasn't scared.

She was pushing her teacher's buttons.
The New Girl refused to leave the room.
The teacher was at her wit's end.
I'd keep an eye on that broom!

The New Girl had a look in her eye.
I don't see this ending well.
Her teacher called the office.
The New Girl answered the bell.

The New Girl had enough.
She bolted out the door.
She took Evil Barney with her.
Say goodbye to that purple dinosaur!

The class got their money's worth.
Welcome to the wild wild west.
Mr. C's class turned into a circus.
P. T. Barnum would be impressed.

Evil Barney had been taken.
The circus had ended.
The Broom was still standing.
The New Girl likely suspended.

On the way home from school that day
I couldn't help feeling bad.
Mr. C really liked Evil Barney.
The New Girl was really REALLY mad!

My feelings were unwarranted
because the very next day,
Evil Barney was back on Mr. C's desk,
making sure the students obey.

The class was disappointed.
A few students let out a groan.
Evil Barney returned from the dead.
Evil Barney reclaimed his throne!

To figure out the mystery
of how Evil Barney survived,
that would mean asking The New Girl,
which seemed dangerous and ill-advised!

So instead we asked Mr. C,
how did you get Evil Barney back?
"Evil Barney has nine lives,
though I don't really keep track."

Now that the circus had left,
we got back to our review.
One student chose to act like a *clown,*
a day he would rue!

The student said he was sorry.
He promised to behave.
Evil Barney was moved to his desk,
a day he would take to his grave.

We were about to take our test
when The New Girl returned.
She went straight to Mr. C's desk.
I doubt her class was adjourned.

She opened her computer,
but before she started working,
she looked around, probably wondering
where Evil Barney was lurking.

The New Girl seemed to be distracted.
She was seemingly confused.
The New Girl almost looked sad.
A ticking time bomb defused?

Her teacher came to get her.
She didn't have permission to leave.
The New Girl has her own set of rules.
Her teacher has a new pet peeve!

Those two were exhausting,
but they entertained the room.
Place your bets on who'll win the battle:
Evil Barney, The New Girl, or the broom?

The New Girl was about to snap.
You could cut the tension with a knife.
Battle lines are being drawn
in this academic strife!

The New Girl approached Mr. C
and whispered in his ear.
Then she confronted The Clown.
He couldn't hide his fear.

She didn't assault him.
The Clown was scared and confused.
She took Evil Barney off his desk.
Mr. C actually seemed amused.

The New Girl walked out the door
with Evil Barney under her arm.
Her teacher was chewing her ear off.
Will Evil Barney buy the farm?

You could've heard a pin drop.
We were baffled by this song and dance.
There was still an elephant in the room.
I think The Clown just wet his pants!

A precedent was established
that was shocking and surprising.
Evil Barney was no longer infamous.
The grassroots of an uprising!

Evil Barney and The New Girl
formed an alliance that day.
The Hellions of Rebellion.
Warriors ... come out and play!

The Rebellion grew in numbers,
The New Girl sticking to her conviction.
Evil Barney was now famous.
Truth is stranger than fiction.

If I hadn't seen it firsthand,
I'd say that you're lying.
Barney dolls were now everywhere!
Both hilarious and horrifying!

Students that were once punished
by holding a doll considered evil
now were part of a movement—
a New Girl's broom-defying upheaval!

Not forgotten in this story
is the teacher with the broom.
She HATED The Rebellion!
As you would probably assume.

The teacher went to administration,
I'm sure with her broom in hand.
She complained about The Rebellion.
The teacher insisted the dolls be banned!

She said, "School is about learning
and rigorous instruction!
Having dolls in the classroom
hinders academic production!"

The principal agreed,
and all the dolls were removed.
That not nothing was something.
Let's just say The New Girl disapproved.

I'm struggling to understand
what the teacher thought she'd accomplish.
The New Girl was on her best behavior
when Evil Barney was her accomplice.

The teacher couldn't see
the forest through the trees.
The New Girl was a pain,
a cure with no disease.

Evil Barney had powers.
Some might call him a sage.
The New Girl was a hellion,
but Evil Barney controlled her rage.

Without Evil Barney,
I expect helter-skelter.
The New Girl will go rogue.
A good time to seek shelter.

The next few days at school
were like learning in a mortuary.
To quote Luna Lovegood, school became
"exceptionally ordinary."

The Barney dolls were silly,
but they made learning kind of fun.
That teacher is sanctimonious!
The New Girl had been outdone.

Our day was at the bottom of the ninth
with two strikes and three balls.
Another school day was wrapping up
when we heard yelling in the halls.

The New Girl was on the run.
I guess I had spoken too soon.
I heard her scream at her teacher
what the teacher could do with her broom!

The circus had returned.
The New Girl slamming a locker.
She came running into our room.
She called her teacher a stalker!

Her teacher and the principal
followed closely behind.
The New Girl went to Mr. C's desk,
both giving her a piece of their mind.

"YOUR BEHAVIOR WON'T BE TOLERATED!"
"WE'VE HAD IT UP TO HERE!"
"YOUR SHENANIGANS NEED TO STOP!"
"YOUR PUNISHMENT WILL BE SEVERE!"

A Hellion of Rebellion,
the *outsider* everyone fears,
The New Girl screamed some things,
then she broke down in tears.

Mr. C had seen enough
and drew a line in the sand.
He handed Evil Barney to her.
Evil Barney took a stand.

Our class watched in awe.
I saw the teacher roll her eyes.
Just like Michael, Jason, and Freddy...
EVIL never really dies!

The New Girl became calm.
She whispered something to Mr. C.
The principal was dumbfounded.
Evil Barney just set her free!

It was hard to figure out
just what the principal was thinking.
She said, "Mr. C, see me in my office.
I think we need to have a meeting."

Mr. C dismissed the class.
The bell had already rung.
The New Girl hadn't thrown in the towel.
Her latest outburst was unsung.

Just a few days later,
our Barney dolls had been returned.
The Hellions of Rebellion were back!
The principal's decision overturned.

The class was ecstatic.
Some of the students actually cheered.
An amusing contradiction
in a school year that was just plain weird!

Mr. C wouldn't elaborate
other than "someone jumped a shark."
Call it a clean sweep.
Evil Barney just hit it out of the park!

Another school year came and went,
just like so many before.
The New Girl learned to *stay gold*
in this modern-day folklore.

You may be wondering
if Evil Barney's reign would resume?
Legend says he rode off into the sunset...
He was last seen riding on a broom.

WHAT YOU TALKIN' 'BOUT, WILLIS?

A glossary is like a mini dictionary at the back of a book. It's an alphabetical list of terms or words that are defined to help the reader better understand the story. The author chooses words he or she feels are uncommon and readers don't hear or see everyday.

An index is a simple key to locating information contained in a book that is usually in alphabetical order at the end of a book.

An appendix is a section or table of additional matter at the end of a book or document.

So you've read this book, and instead of seeing a glossary, index, or appendix ... you see "What You Talkin' 'bout, Willis?" WHO DOES THAT?

I have to take you back to a time long ago. From 1978 to 1986, there was a TV show called *Diff'rent Strokes.* It was about two kids from Harlem. Their mother was a housekeeper for a rich guy named Phillip Drummond. The mother passes away, and Mr. Drummond adopts the two boys, Arnold and Willis Jackson. It was a half-hour situation comedy (sitcom).

Whenever Willis, the older brother, would say something that Arnold, the younger brother, didn't understand, Arnold would say, "What you talkin' 'bout, Willis?" This became a famous catchphrase throughout the '80s. Everybody was saying it!

Catchphrases are well-known sentences or phrases. They're usually associated with a famous person.

Here are a few examples. If you don't know them, I bet your parents or grandparents do!

“Dyn-o-mite!” —J. J. Evans, *Good Times*

“Marcia, Marcia, Marcia!” —Jan Brady, *The Brady Bunch*

“You got it, dude.” —Michelle Tanner, *Full House*

“Can you smelllll ... what the rock ... is cookin’?”
—WWE wrestler and actor Dwayne (The Rock) Johnson

“Bazinga!” —Sheldon Cooper, *The Big Bang Theory*

“D’oh!” —Homer Simpson, *The Simpsons*

The twelve stories you read were filled with a LOT of things! There was alliteration, allusion, assonance, consonance, hyperbole, idioms, imagery, inferences, internal rhymes, irony, metaphors, onomatopoeia, paradox, personification, rhymes, similes, stanzas, adjectives, nouns, pronouns, verbs, adverbs, proverbs, small words, big words, nice words, mean words, fake curse words, actual curse words, old words, new words, words that make you look smart if you use them in a sentence, words that make you look not so smart if you use them in a sentence, words that can show up on state tests, words that can make you laugh, words that can make you cry, hidden messages, hidden meanings, and things you will only find if you read between the lines.

Try reading "What You Talkin' 'bout, Willis?" and then rereading the stories. I bet you find something different the second time!

adjective: Describes a noun. *You have an* **ugly** *hat.*

adverb: Modifies adjectives or other adverbs. *He runs* ***slowly***.

alliteration: The repetition of identical consonant sounds. *She sells seashells by the seashore.*

allusion: Unacknowledged reference the author assumes the reader will recognize.

anaphora: The reptition of a word or words at the start of several lines of poetry. Used to emphasize an idea or emotion.

antagonist: The character in a story who goes against the protagonist and is often considered the villain.

assonance: The repetition of identical vowel sounds. *L**u**mpy, b**u**mpy, gr**u**mpy...*

consonance: Repetition of sounds produced by consonants. ***Bl**ade, **bl**ood, **bl**ow...*

hyperbole: Exaggerating characteristics or claims not to be taken seriously. *"My feet are killing me!"*

idiom: Phrase that is different than its literal meaning. *"She let the cat out of the bag."*

imagery: Images created by the words you're reading using your five senses.

implied metaphor: A type of metaphor that compares two things that are not alike without actually mentioning one of those things. "The leaves were fluttering in the breeze" (compares leaves to butterflies).

inference: A conclusion reached on the basis of evidence and reasoning.

internal rhyme: A rhyme that is exact. *Dreary, weary...*

metaphor: Comparing two things that are not alike. You cannot use *like* or *as. My mom is a bear when she wakes up!*

noun: Person, place, thing, or idea.

onomatopoeia: Words used to represent sounds. *Buzz, woosh, vroom...*

paradox: A contradictory statement that turns out to be true.

personification: Giving human characteristics to things that are not human.

pronoun: Replace nouns. *He, she, they, them.*

protagonist: The main character in a story and often the hero.

proverb: A short saying that is an obvious truth. *Two wrongs don't make a right.*

rhyme: The repetition of identical concluding syllables in different words, most often at the ends of lines.

simile: Comparing two things that are not alike using *like* or *as*. *My mom is* like *a bear when she wakes up.*

stanza: A group of lines forming the basic structure of a poem.

verb: A word that shows action. *Run, jump, swim...*

YOU DON'T KNOW WHAT YOU DON'T KNOW

monkey off my back

(idiom) To take care of something that has been bothering you once and for all.

slip of the tongue

(idiom) To say something you shouldn't have.

song and dance

(idiom) An elaborate explanation of something usually trying to get yourself out of trouble or to justify something.

befuddled

(verb) Unable to focus or think clearly.

awkward

(adjective) Causing difficulty or hard to deal with.

sweep under the rug

(idiom) To ignore, deny, or conceal something.

a feather in the hand is better than two birds in the sky

(proverb) It is better to have something than nothing at all.

fainthearted
(adjective) Lacking courage or bravery.

rigorous
(adjective) Extremely thorough, exhaustive, or accurate. Teachers LOVE this term!

golden rule
(noun) Treat others how you want to be treated.

ruse
(noun) An action intending to deceive; a trick.

walk a day in their shoes
(idiom) Trying to understand what someone is dealing with.

judge a book by its cover
(idiom) Metaphorical phrase meaning outward appearance doesn't always tell you the story.

a lot on our plate
(idiom) Overwhelmed or have a lot to deal with.

debate
(noun) A formal discussion about a topic where two or more people each have a different opinion.

helicopter mom

(noun) A parent who goes over the top getting involved in every detail of their child's business.

agitated

(adjective) Feeling upset, nervous, or troubled.

scheme

(noun) A large-scale plan to put one's own ideas or beliefs into action.

hearsay

(noun) Rumor.

by hook or by crook

(idiom) To do something by any means necessary.

dispel

(verb) Make a doubt, feeling, or belief about something disappear.

get your feet wet

(idiom) To gain experience with something.

cold as ice

(idiom) A person who doesn't show any emotion; very serious.

resting grumpy face (RGF)
(noun) Someone who always looks "mad" even if they're not.

eavesdropping
(verb) Secretly listening to a conversation.

frazzled
(verb) Feeling completely exhausted or worn out.

spin
(noun) Taking a negative event and making it seem more positive.

a lightbulb went off in my head
(idiom) You suddenly figure something out.

paradox
(noun) An absurd statement that, when further investigated or explained, turns out to be true.

ball is in his court
(idiom) It's his turn to do something.

put this story to bed
(idiom) To end the story.

hindsight is 20/20
(proverb) It's easy to know what you should've done after you've made a mistake.

stirring the pot
(idiom) To agitate or cause problems in a situation.

covert operation
(noun) A secret military operation.

wielding
(verb) Holding a knife in a way that it appears you are going to use it for something.

HONOR AMONG THIEVES

complied
(verb) Do what someone wants you to do.

abide
(verb) Follow a rule or expectation.

attest
(verb) To be a witness to.

another brick in the wall
(idiom) You're just another student among hundreds of others.

insidious
(adjective) Someone (or something) that works in a subtle or sly way with harmful effects or intent.

hideous
(adjective) Ugly or disgusting to look at.

profusely
(adverb) To do in large amounts.

fell on deaf ears
(idiom) To be ignored.

flip my lid
(idiom) Get really mad.

provoke
(verb) Deliberately make (someone) annoyed or angry.

transparent
(adjective) Easy to detect what someone is up to; see through what they're up to.

movement break
(noun) A term some schools have used that allow certain students who struggle with focusing, sitting still, or appropriate classroom behavior to take a "break" from the normal classroom routine and instruction.

reprieve
(noun) A cancellation or postponement of a punishment.

blind eye
(idiom) To pretend not to notice something.

profound
(adjective) Very intense or extreme.

underground
(noun) You are doing something that is hidden or concealed from others. *"Harriet Tubman started the Underground Railroad to help slaves in the South escape to the North."*

panic attack
(noun) The sudden onset of intense fear.

juggernaut
(noun) An overwhelming or overpowering force.

drinking the Kool-Aid
When somebody wants you to think and/or act in a certain way that may be different than how you should or what you are accustomed to.

swan song
(noun) Metaphorical phrase for a final gesture or action before the end of something.

fell down a hole chasing a white rabbit
(metaphor) This comes from the book *Alice In Wonderland.* Falling down the hole means you can't stop thinking about something (obsessing over). The white rabbit represents chasing something you can't seem to achieve.

watershed moment
(noun) A turning point after which things will never be the same.

paradigm shift
(noun) Change in the usual way of thinking.

chagrin
(noun) Distress or embarrassment at having failed or been humiliated.

card up my sleeve
(idiom) Have an advantage that someone doesn't know about.

not bat an eye
(idiom) You are not surprised at all by something that you've heard or that has happened.

what goes around comes around
(proverb) Your actions (good or bad) will always come back to you; karma.

dumbfounded
(verb) Completely amazed by something.

redemption
(noun) Being saved from something that is evil.

paper tiger
(noun) Refers to someone who at first seems to be powerful, but as you look closer, you realize they are completely powerless.

Cheshire grin
(noun) Related to the Cheshire Cat, from the book *Alice In Wonderland.* It means to smile big and with a little bit of an attitude and sarcasm.

eyes are like daggers
(simile) Trying to intimidate someone just by looking at them.

hanging by a thread
(idiom) To be in a risky or unstable situation.

aghast
(adjective) Filled with horror or shock.

burlesque

(noun) A funny, exaggerated situation; a parody.

symbiotic

(adjective) Mutually beneficial relationship between different people.

thick as thieves

(idiom) Two people who are very close and reliant on each other.

checkmate

(noun) When playing the game chess, the opponent's king has no move left to make and, therefore, has been defeated and the game is over.

WHERE EAGLES DARE

beseeching

(verb) To beg or implore.

hazmat suit

(noun) Whole-body outfit worn to protect against hazardous material.

beggars can't be choosers

(proverb) Someone with no other options has to be OK with what is offered.

urinal cake
(noun) A disinfectant block placed by the drain of a urinal used to sanitize and deodorize. *Makes the pee smell go away...*

an eagle has landed
(idiom) A mission has been completed.

chitchat
(noun) Talking, especially small talk or gossip.

cleared the air
(idiom) Talked about something that needed to be talked about.

commode
(noun) Another name for a toilet.

ducks in a row
(idiom) To get organized and to have things figured out.

fork in the road
(metaphor) A deciding moment in your life. A big decision to be made.

THE SNOWBALL EFFECT

goes to eleven
(pop culture reference) It means really REALLY loud! It's a reference from the movie *Spinal Tap.* Guitar amplifiers at full volume only go to ten, so imagine if it went to eleven!

off her rocker
(idiom) Crazy.

mean mugging
(verb) Slang term for someone giving you a dirty look.

rat in a cage
(idiom) Feeling trapped in a situation.

unfounded
(adjective) Can't prove something to be a fact.

the roads were an ice rink
(metaphor) The roads were very slippery because of the ice.

rub salt on a wound
(idiom) To make a bad situation even worse.

flimflam
(noun) Nonsense, deception, or to swindle.

grudgingly
(adverb) Doing something you don't really want to do.

math-targeted instruction
Another way of saying you're doing extra math! It most commonly occurs right before a test to prepare and right after a test to revisit skills that weren't mastered.

disco
(noun) Popular dance music and way of dancing from way back in the 1970s.

out of the blue
(metaphor) Without warning.

the eleventh hour
(noun) Doing something at the last possible moment.

throwing in the towel
(idiom) To give up.

blankety-blank
(adjective) It represents words that should NOT be said in school. You can decide what words they are!

succumbed
(verb) When you give in to something.

MARVELOUS MERCHISTON

add fuel to the fire
(idiom) Make a situation even worse.

sorcerer
(noun) Another name for a wizard.

elicited
(verb) To gain a reaction.

occult
(noun) Supernatural and mystical beliefs and powers.

black magic
(noun) Magic or supernatural powers used for evil or selfish purposes.

outside the box
(metaphor) Think differently from others and from a new perspective.

sly as a fox
(idiom) Exceptionally clever and sometimes sneaky.

physicist
(noun) An expert in studying and understanding physics.

astronomer
(noun) A scientist that focuses on studies outside of the Earth (e.g., stars, moon, planets).

mathematician
(noun) An expert or student of math.

macabre *(muh-KAB)*
(adjective) Something disturbing and horrifying.

thingamabob
(noun) Referring to something when you aren't sure what it is.

logarithm(s)
(noun) A quantity representing the power to which a fixed number (the base) must be raised to produce a given number. *(It's really not as bad as it sounds...)*

Napier's bones
(noun) An early way to make multiplication and division easier using bone or ivory. Invented by John Napier.

lattice method
(noun) A method of multiplying bigger numbers.

inept
(adjective) Lacking the ability to do something.

shifty
(adjective) Sneaky or deceitful.

booster
(noun) Slang term for someone who steals something.

clairvoyant
(adjective) The ability to see what others cannot.

absurd
(adjective) Dumb or extremely silly.

deceitful
(adjective) Not being honest.

restraint
(noun) Holding back from doing something.

reprimanded
(verb) Get in trouble for something; consequences.

conscience
(noun) An inner feeling you have about your behavior being right or wrong.

caught red-handed
(idiom) Getting caught in the act of doing something.

schmuck
(noun) Foolish, stupid, or unlikeable person.

piece of his mind
(idiom) Tell someone what you really think of them.

inebriated
(noun) When you drink too much alcohol and you become drunk.

three sheets to the wind
(idiom) To be drunk.

raise a white flag
(idiom) Give up a fight; surrender.

DARK SIDE OF THE WALL

compliance
(noun) Conforming to others or doing as they wish.

taunt
(verb) To tease.

uncharted waters
(idiom) Something new and unknown.

calm before the storm
(idiom) When things are quiet just before they get out of control.

abyss
(noun) A nearly impossible situation to deal with; a space so wide or deep that it can't be measured.

stuck in between a rock and a hard place
(idiom) Choosing between two equally difficult choices.

save face
(idiom) Keep from being embarrassed or humiliated.

scrawl
(noun) Careless, sloppy, hurried handwriting.

graffiti
(noun) Writing or drawings scribbled, scratched, or sprayed illicitly on a wall or other surface in a public place.

Elvis
(noun) Famous singer, actor, and entertainer.

Elvis has left the building
(idiom) The show is over.

camel and some straw

(idiom) The straw that broke the camel's back means the final thing that happens to cause a huge reaction.

raised a red flag

(idiom) Bring awareness to something.

culprit

(noun) Someone responsible for a crime.

unsympathetic

(adjective) Showing no sympathy.

problematic

(adjective) Presenting a problem or difficulty.

ascertain

(verb) To find something out for sure.

obscene

(adjective) Offensive, disgusting, or even repugnant.

floating without a paddle up a certain creek

(idiom) Also: Up a creek without a paddle. In a troublesome situation.

hat trick

(noun) When one player scores three goals in a soccer or hockey game.

thrown under the bus
(idiom) Go against someone or turn on someone for personal gain.

exonerated
(verb) Being found innocent of wrongdoing.

dog and pony show
(noun) Over the top and elaborate display or performance.

HOW WAS YOUR DAY?

smoke and mirrors
(idiom) Hiding the truth of a situation by being misleading.

coerced
(verb) Get someone to do something, even by force.

persistent
(adjective) Not giving up on something until you get what you want.

insistent
(adjective) Demanding something and not taking "no" for an answer.

perplexed
(verb) Being completely confused by something.

shady
(adjective) Someone that isn't trustworthy.

suspect
(verb) Thought to be guilty of bad behavior or a crime.

just stepped in something
(idiom) Put yourself in a bad situation.

mind is racing
(idiom) Can't stop thinking about something.

devil's advocate
(noun) To argue against something ... point/counter-point.

TWO FINGERS FOR YOU

due diligence
(noun) To avoid problems by taking care of all aspects of something.

adieu
(noun) Goodbye.

deranged
(adjective) Mad or insane.

Severus Snape
(noun) A wizard from the Harry Potter books.

Thing One and Thing Two
(nouns) Two characters that were troublemakers in the Dr. Seuss book *The Cat in the Hat.*

abhor
(verb) Regard something with hatred and disgust.

ears will be burning
(idiom) Someone feels that someone is talking about them.

avant-garde
(noun) Something considered new and experimental.

under my skin
(idiom) Someone is irritating you.

construe
(verb) Interpret a word or action in a particular way.

crucifix
(noun) A cross.

through the roof
(idiom) To become very angry or upset.

two cents
(idiom) Offer your opinion.

pondering
(verb) Thinking about something carefully.

sixth sense
(noun) Power of perception, unlike your other five senses.

King's X
(noun) In kids games, a term to call truce and grant you temporary immunity from something. When you cross your fingers, you aren't held accountable.

dodged a bullet
(idiom) Avoid a bad situation.

spill the beans
(idiom) Reveal secret information unintentionally or indiscreetly.

ballistic (going ballistic)
(adjective) Extremely upset or angry.

pessimistic
(adjective) Believing the worst will happen.

all cards on the table
(idiom) To be fully honest about something.

catch-22
(noun) A situation when you have to make a choice and neither choice is good.

deer in headlights
(idiom) So frightened you can't move or make a decision.

solace
(noun) To find comfort in a stressful situation.

flawless
(adjective) Do something perfectly.

foreboding
(noun/adjective) To imply something is bad.

albatross
(noun/adjective) Something that causes concern or anxiety.

end of my rope
(idiom) Having no strength or patience left.

come clean
(idiom) Tell the truth.

on the shelf
(idiom) Something on hold or not happening.

talk trash
(noun) To say things that aren't necessarily true to get a reaction or get someone off their game.

rapport (RUH-poor)
(noun) Having a feeling of relation or connection.

avenged sevenfold
(noun) To get even for something.

push the envelope
(idiom) To push the limits of something.

dug a hole
(idiom) To put yourself into a difficult situation.

walking a tightrope
(idiom) Doing something that is difficult to do.

peace of mind
(noun) Mental state of being calm, free from worry and guilt.

glass is half full
(metaphor) An expression that determines the attitude you have toward something. If you look at a situation and only see the challenges and faults with it, the glass is half empty. If you look at a situation and see the possibilities or opportunities, the glass is half full. It's how you perceive a situation.

clincher
(noun) Something or someone that settles a situation conclusively.

ace in the hole
(idiom) Something you keep hidden until the last minute that works to your advantage.

means to an end
(idiom) Something you do only to provide a desired result.

audacious
(adjective) A willingness to take surprisingly bold risks.

hellacious
(adjective) Very bad or overwhelming.

bark is worse than her bite
(idiom) Someone is not as mean as they seem to be and is not as a bad as his or her threats.

live by the sword, die by the sword
(proverb) What goes around comes around, treat others how you expect to be treated, and your actions will come back to you ... *karma.*

lying in wait
(idiom) To wait for just the right moment to attack or ambush someone.

barrage
(noun) An overwhelming outpouring of words.

slippery slope
(idiom) A dangerous and irreversible course of action.

blood boiling
(idiom) Extremely mad.

seeing red
(idiom) Full of anger.

tailspin
(verb) Become out of control.

John McClane and *Die Hard*
John McClane was the name of the main character in a popular '80s movie called *Die Hard.* The movie is about a bunch of bad guys that take over a building and hold people hostage. John McClane is a cop that shows up

unexpectedly to surprise his wife at the Christmas work party. He ends up having to save the day. Alan Rickman was the actor that played the role of the bad guy (Hans Gruber) and is also the actor that was Severus Snape in the Harry Potter movies.

beeline
(noun) To go in a straight line.

obedient
(adjective) Being willing to do what someone tells you to do.

walk over his grave
(idiom) To shudder or shake uncontrollably because of fear.

snide
(adjective) Doing something in a mocking or derogatory way.

capisce *(KUH-peesh)*
(exclamation) It means, do you understand?

hit a snag
(idiom) To run into a problem.

afterglow
(noun) Good feelings that remain from a positive experience.

white on rice
(idiom) That you are on top of a situation.

run for the hills
(idiom) To flee or to run.

dead in his tracks
(idiom) To stop very suddenly.

will
(noun) The legal written wishes of someone that determines what happens with their stuff after they die.

out of hand
(idiom) When things are no longer under control.

leniency
(noun) Showing mercy or more tolerance than expected.

third degree
(noun) Long and hard questioning to get an answer and the truth.

mistrial
(noun) When a jury can't agree on a verdict about a case.

back of his hand
(adjective) Making a comment that is insincere.

in the hole
(noun) Solitary confinement in prison. Sometimes it was located under the prison floor.

gloating
(verb) Bragging about an accomplishment.

put in our place
(idiom) To make aware that someone is not as special or important as they think they are.

came with a price
(idiom) An action that brings with it an unwanted consequence.

jeer
(verb) To make rude and mocking comments.

lie through his teeth
(idiom) Not being truthful, dishonest.

pushing up daisies
(idiom) To be dead and buried.

snarky
(adjective) Being sarcastic and mocking.

upperhand

(noun) To have an advantage in a situation.

talk smack

(verb) To be intentionally insulting to annoy someone.

no-man's-land

(noun) A place that is undesirable.

death wish

(noun) To do something extremely dangerous.

cliché

(noun) Overuse of something, lacking an original thought.

get the picture

(idiom) To understand what is going on without anything having to be said.

LIE CHEAT STEAL INTRODUCTION

Beetlejuice

Famous movie character from the '80s, played by Michael Keaton, who caused trouble for people who would summon him by saying his name three times.

The Simpsons
The longest-running TV show and animated series, first aired in 1989.

horticulturist
(noun) An expert in gardening and cultivation.

assert
(verb) To state a fact or to show confidence.

venomous
(adjective) Vicious, spiteful, or mean-spirited language.

obligatory
(adjective) Legally required or a customary routine.

accredited
(adjective) Officially recognized or authorized.

LIE

explicit
(adjective) Not appropriate for everybody; too extreme.

threw shade
(idiom) Disrespecting someone.

fester
(verb) A negative feeling keeps growing, especially when you don't do anything about it.

exquisite
(adjective) Extremely beautiful; perfect.

take the bull by the horns
(idiom) Taking charge in a difficult situation.

extortion
(noun) Getting something through force or threats.

going the extra mile
(idiom) Doing more than is required.

surly
(adjective) Bad-tempered or unfriendly.

gather my bearings
(idiom) To figure out your situation.

CHEAT

takes the cake
(idiom) The best at something.

hit the fan

(idiom) Big problems arise.

refuge

(noun) Being safe or sheltered in a dangerous or bad situation.

wreaking havoc

(verb) Causing problems; causing disruption or damage.

notorious

(adjective) Well known for doing something bad or being bad.

daunting

(adjective) Too difficult or scary to deal with.

sleuth

(noun) A detective.

forsake

(verb) To abandon.

STEAL

weathering the storm

(idiom) To deal with a difficult situation.

curiosity killed the cat
(idiom) Worrying about other people and what they're doing could get you into trouble.

precarious
(adjective) A dangerous or insecure position.

monkey wrench
(verb) To cause disruption.

regime
(noun) A system of rules, authority, or government.

at wit's end
(idiom) No more patience.

P. T. Barnum
Famous for his three-ring traveling circus. The Ringling Brothers Barnum & Bailey Traveling Circus started in the early 1900s and lasted until 2017.

rue
(verb) To regret.

adjourned
(verb) To end a meeting.

pet peeve
(noun) Something you find annoying.

buy the farm
(idiom) To die.

elephant in the room
(idiom) A question that needs to be answered but nobody wants to address it because it could feel uncomfortable or be awkward.

Warriors ... come out and play
A famous line from the movie *The Warriors* that came out in 1979. It means to challenge someone.

precedent
(noun) Something that happens that becomes an example of how something is achieved.

infamous
(adjective) Well known for doing something bad.

conviction
(noun) A strong belief or opinion.

upheaval
(noun) A sudden and abrupt change in something.

accomplice
(noun) A person who helps you commit a crime.

sage
(noun) Someone who is wise.

go rogue
(figure of speech) Behaving erratically and refusing to conform.

helter-skelter
(adjective) To do something in a chaotic, out-of-control way.

mortuary
(noun) A funeral home.

Luna Lovegood
A character from the Harry Potter series.

sanctimonious
(adjective) Feeling morally superior to others.

unsung
(adjective) Not celebrated or acknowledged.

jumping the shark
(idiom) When something is accomplished (a goal), and then things starts to decline in some way.

stay gold

A famous poem by Robert Frost, "Nothing Gold Can Stay," referred to in the movie *The Outsiders.* Stay gold means to not conform, stay true to who you are, and know that all good things will come to an end someday.

ABOUT THE AUTHOR

Jeff Chartier was a Title 1 public school teacher for twenty-five years. Mr. C has won various awards including the Lincoln Airport Authority Classroom Coach of the Week, the *Lincoln Journal Star* A+ Educator Award, the Alltel Outstanding Education Award, and the Rotary Club Teacher of the Month.

Mr. C has had the privilege of teaching the most amazing students from all over the world. He has had over fourteen different languages spoken in his classrooms.

Somewhere during that time, Mr. C started telling stories to make his lessons more meaningful to and impactful on his students. The stories have been used to motivate students to come in before and after school for extra support, to stay out of trouble, to provide a deeper understanding of an objective, and sometimes ... just to get them to show up to school! This book includes just a few of those stories.

Mr. C has spoken at schools, to youth groups, and to college students aspiring to be teachers. When he isn't teaching or writing, he can be found spending time with his wife and two kids, riding his bicycle out on some gravel road, or playing in the '80s tribute band AMFM.

If you want to connect with Mr. C, you can visit his website at jeffchartierauthor.com or email him at jeffchartier228@gmail.com.

"It's the one thing you can control. You are responsible for how people remember you—or don't. So don't take it lightly."

—Kobe Bryant

CPSIA information can be obtained
at www.ICGtesting.com
Printed in the USA
LVHW020725240721
693345LV00004B/9